Ice

'A bridge between past and present'

Ken Brown

First published in the United Kingdom in 2023 by
The Choir Press

ISBN 978-1-78963-377-1

Ice is a work of fiction. However, the 1867 disaster in Regents Park, about which the story revolves, was a real event. Also real was the planting of a commemorative oak on Primrose Hill. Any resemblance to actual persons, living or dead, is unintentional and purely coincidental. Some long-standing institutions, agencies and public offices may be mentioned to create scenery for the purposes of the story.

Thanks to

Anita Brayford for her patient help throughout with research,
editing and applied IT skills.

Rose Niland Smith whose practical help made this book
possible and whose lifelong daily journal inspired Jean's diary.

Roger Burfield for his aviation advice.

Acknowledgements

Primrose Hill Remembered
Published by The Friends of Chalk Farm Library

Useful Toil
Edited by John Burnett
Allen Lane
Penguin Books Ltd.

Provided inspiration and colour

CHAPTER ONE
– England 1942

E arly on 18 February, Pilot Officer Alec Kirk and Sergeant Colin Davies walked out of the training school classroom block at Hullavington just as the sun was dispersing the light overnight mist. Their briefing, just concluded, had been straightforward. A zig-zag course, practising simple navigational skills at two and a half thousand feet heading overall due north. This was to be Davies's fifth flight and the sheer thrill of flight hadn't abated. He felt privileged to have been selected for pilot training. Many of the pilots joining the RAF had previous flying experience at clubs frequented by well-off families. No such opportunities had been available to him in Port Talbot where his father laboured daily in the steelworks. So even mundane routine tasks thrilled him just as long as they meant he could be near an aeroplane. He'd actually asked Kirk following their most recent lesson whether, after his hundreds of flying hours, he still felt that excitement. Kirk had paused, smiling, and replied that if ever he lost that feeling he would give up flying. He then went on to emphasise the constant awareness required, which meant that the gifts of flight were always conditional. There were plenty of wrecked aircraft around to illustrate the point.

'You might be distracted enough to forget to check the windsock – come in to land downwind. It happens. You might try taking off with coarse prop setting. That happens. Both can kill you or wreck your aircraft.'

His advice, though serious, had been delivered with an edge of wry humour. Today was different. As the two men crunched across the dew-laden grass to the Miles Trainer, a bulky looking monoplane that Davies already loved, not a word was spoken. Kirk looked grim and through the pre-flight checks spoke only when necessary. Davies wasn't going to make inquiries as to his instructor's state of mind. After two years of war bad news of one sort or another was frequent and Kirk's mood could well be due to an unwelcome telegram or telephone call. It is doubtful anyway that Kirk would have responded. He had told no one about the message he had received the previous evening, telling him that his younger brother was missing.

Steve had chosen to go to sea five years earlier when no one could have predicted the terror of Atlantic convoys. On his last shore leave he had described to his brother the unrelenting fear of attack that dominated the minds of the sailors aboard the ships crossing the Atlantic, whether escorted or not. Information was hard to get due to security concerns but Kirk knew which ship Steve had sailed on and that *MV Savona* had not arrived in port after losing touch with her convoy. In fact, a worn and overheated bearing had caused the ship to lose speed and fall behind, an easy target for U 903. A single torpedo was enough to sink the vessel and she and her valuable cargo of refrigerated food and copper disappeared in minutes with no survivors observed by the submarine. Kirk, of course, knew nothing of this, but with no definite information Kirk had to face the possibility of Steve's death.

His feelings as he prepared for this morning's flight were a mixture of shock and anger. Whereas he himself had had the chance to fight, merchant seamen sailing in unarmed ships to keep Britain alive were being slaughtered daily. All the more reason to get on with the job then. The sergeant was a promising trainee and needed little guidance on the checks, so with his instructor so quiet, Davies could easily imagine that he was to fly solo. He called out to the attending aircraftsman that the magneto was switched off and watched as the propeller swung round a few times, priming the engine with fuel. Then with magneto on, one swing brought the engine to life with a roar. They rolled out to the take-off runway and Davies went over take-off procedures in his mind several times. Then, at a word from Kirk, came the moments of exhilaration as the brakes were released and surging power accelerated them along the runway. The lack of headwind made take off more laborious than he'd previously experienced but once airborne, the climb to their operational height went smoothly. The countryside below was sharply defined as the last of the haziness vanished. It was beautiful. Davies had to force himself not to sing with joy. He had little difficulty picking out landmarks and roads on their to and fro course and there were few comments from Kirk over the intercom.

A little later and twenty-five miles to the north, Flying Officer Daniel Pledger and Pilot Officer Keith Griffin were completing checks on their Tiger Moth at the Flying Instructors' School, Staverton. Pledger was keeping a close eye on his student to make sure no slackness had crept in during his three years of flying. Griffin himself was looking forward to today's session. He was confident that he would make a good instructor but knew he had to convince Pledger that his flying skills were up to scratch. Even so he was hoping for some exciting moves in the Moth. It would make a change from high-speed combat in a Spitfire. Shot down in the English Channel once, Griffin took nothing for granted and Pledger was happy with his thoroughness. Taking off into the bright morning air, the war seemed far away to them both.

They went through a series of spins and rolls which Griffin executed well. Pledger then ordered a slow level course for several minutes. 'Make your trainees do this perfectly in different conditions and they'll have a good basis for any manoeuvres,' Pledger said.

Neither aviator noticed a single monoplane high above them and at some distance to their rear. Had they done so they might have seen it change course and start towards them.

The Miles Trainer had by this time arrived within sight of Cheltenham. Davies had flown the planned erratic course without incident, keeping altitude well on most of the turns. Kirk was satisfied and was about to order the return setting when he was distracted by a chance glimpse of a biplane some distance from and lower than the Miles. The Tiger Moth had begun level flight after a spell of aerobatics.

Kirk saw an opportunity to carry out an unscheduled practice attack and for the first time that day forgot about his brother. The Moth was cruising at an angle to the sun and Kirk told Davies to climb and turn to put the sun directly behind then to start a shallow dive on the biplane as if attacking.

'I'll take over when we're close,' shouted Kirk.

As they descended, picking up speed, Kirk was again impressed by Davies' ability. He had anticipated the Moth's position so well that had the situation been real, they would have been in a good position to press home the attack. As they closed in Kirk took the controls and began to climb. Although he doubted that the Moth's crew were aware of the Miles, he planned to overfly the biplane to its right. He knew this was risky and, had he survived, would have admitted recklessness.

Meanwhile, in the Tiger Moth, the shadow of the monoplane flashed over the two pilots. To Griffin, with reactions primed by his many combat sorties, this signalled an enemy attack, and with no thought for his instructor he took immediate evasive action. The aircraft climbed sharply, rolling to the right. Kirk's last seconds passed in shock and disbelief as the Moth reared into view. The Miles tore into the upper body of the small biplane. Its propeller shattering as it hit the fuselage. Pledger and Griffin were killed instantly as the heavy body of the monoplane ploughed along the top of their aircraft. The upper wing of the Moth struck the cockpit covers of the Miles, rendering escape impossible. The Moth's engine screamed at full throttle for a few seconds and the resulting thrust forced the two wrecked planes apart. Spinning away from each other, they fell in spirals, smashing into the ground over one hundred metres apart. Apart from a few creaks from the wreckage, the countryside returned to its usual silence. Two land girls ran towards the remains and a youth delivering telegrams dismounted his bicycle at the nearby crossroads.

In the Atlantic U-Boats hunted fresh targets. In the Soviet Union a German army was moving towards its doom at Stalingrad. America was ponderously gearing up to join the war following the attack on Pearl Harbour and a British army was in retreat across North Africa. Kirk's brother, Steve, had survived the sinking of *MV Savona* and was on his way home.

CHAPTER TWO
– Gloucester 2017

H e'd thought at first that the staff room was empty and that Reg
Saxton, an elderly history teacher, was delivering his talk to the
assembled furniture.

'Ah, here's another young person who won't remember it,' he
announced as Peter entered.

'I was just telling Miss ... um ... Miss ...'

'Copeland,' supplied a voice from behind a pile of boxes and papers.

So she is here, thought Peter, relieved.

'Yes, telling Miss Copeland about the bad old days when you could
hardly see across the room for tobacco fug. Of course we were used to
it. It was everywhere – pubs, cinemas, even restaurants.'

'It's a wonder any of you survived,' said Peter.

Reg paused for a moment to give Peter a hard look.

'A lot didn't,' he said gloomily and trudged out of the room.

There was a giggle behind the boxes.

'Just when I was dying for a smoke.'

Peter walked over as the owner of the voice stood up and held out
her hand.

'I'm sorry I didn't introduce myself properly yesterday. I'm Julie and
you, I know, are Peter Joy, organiser of the Science Group, am I right?'

'Guilty, I'm afraid. Or so some would say.'

Julie gave him a quick quizzical look but let his comment pass.

'Could you hang on for a minute while I finish this collating? I'm
afraid I've got a bit behind.'

Peter was in no hurry and even had he been he would have
postponed most other arrangements. He was intrigued and pleased that
a modern language teacher had inquired about the Science Group.
Elmbridge Academy was a large school and during the short time Julie

had been teaching there Peter had only ever exchanged an occasional good morning with her. Yet she had managed, during a brief corridor encounter yesterday, to arrange this meeting.

He walked slowly over to a window and watched the stragglers leaving. Most students wore backpacks but some were carrying items of one sort or another in their hands and Peter was reminded of one of the ideas put forward at the Science Group. You could pick up a briefcase, say, and walk for miles never giving it a thought yet never relinquishing your grip. How was that, and what would it take to make you let go? Would a shock make you tighten or loosen your hold? It may have been a trivial question but there was clearly an enquiring mind behind it. Peter had been surprised by many of the topics suggested at the group.

His thoughts were interrupted by some hefty thumps, which he assumed signalled the completion of Julie's tasks.

'Right, free at last,' she said, walking over to join Peter at the window.

Peter pulled up a chair for her and sat down opposite.

'OK, the Science Group. What has interested you?'

'Well, I only heard about it a couple of weeks ago. From a student who told me about this Selwood guy who's going to visit the school. In particular, a theory about memory had appealed to this student and he was wondering whether it could be possible to absorb a language without all the hard work of actually learning it. If that were so it would perhaps affect my employment prospects. I was a bit concerned.'

Peter had come across this idea several times recently while discussing Rowan Selwood's work with students. A hypothesis of his being that memory is not stored in the brain but in otherwise undetectable fields.

'That's how I heard about his book,' Julie continued. 'I bought it at once and I'm halfway through it. Fascinating. The idea that beliefs inherited from earlier philosophies but never proved scientifically should be challenged. Obviously I'm going to be particularly interested in the memory bits. Learning languages is very memory orientated of course, though there's a lot more to it.'

'Yes, and for that very reason the idea of absorbing languages effortlessly is probably wishful thinking. I don't think you'll be out of a job yet,' said Peter.

'Oh, but I got the impression that Selwood is advocating a broad, open-mindedness to science.'

'Caught out, I see,' said Peter ruefully. 'Well if you think of perception, memory and imagination as a triangle linked by information, which I find is a useful way of thinking, then even if it were possible to transfer information from one person to another by hitherto unknown means, the complexity and rules of a language in its cultural setting go beyond mere memory, don't you think? Also you might end up with a load of words and not know what any of them meant.'

'Maybe, but what about other things?' Julie was not going to let her new enthusiasm get dampened. 'Things like telepathy, people getting glimpses of past lives. Stuff like that. I could imagine that being associated with memories floating around.'

Peter was impressed. 'I think by the sound of it you'd better come to hear Selwood's talk.'

'Wonderful – I thought you'd never ask. I'll be there.'

'Good. I must tell you though that a few of my departmental colleagues disapprove of the visit.'

'Oh?'

'They believe students should be concentrating on the syllabus – not be distracted by highly speculative ideas.'

'I'd better keep quiet then, but I'm looking forward to it.'

Julie balanced her boxes and walked to the door.

'By the way,' said Peter, 'earlier – were you?'

Julie thought for two seconds.

'Oh that? Dying for a smoke? Yes, and still am.'

Peter held open the door and Julie tottered through.

'Can I take some of that?'

'No. I'm nicely balanced thanks. In some ways anyway.'

'What about doors?'

'Oh, someone'll be there. Bye,' she replied gaily.

Peter was left, for some reason, feeling happier than he had been all week.

CHAPTER THREE

———◆———

Peter failed to see Julie during the following week but she surprised him by turning up on the next Thursday for the Science Group meeting held in one of the laboratories. As the students arrived he had time to explain the group's origins. It had been started, with Peter's help, by a keen sixth former who had read and been inspired by Selwood's book, *Science: Quest and Question*, which argued forcibly for more open and imaginative views of science than those held by many scientists. Students attending the group were encouraged to read the book and Peter had found that those who had done so were often motivated to come up with interesting ideas and projects. Some of these were quite original, and simple experiments could be designed to explore them at the Thursday meetings. Whether through these or the many animated discussions, the students were free to be creative and imaginative away from the curriculum.

'Today we are carrying out an experiment,' Peter told Julie. 'You'll be amused to hear that it involves the activities of a few woodlice. Don't worry though. No creatures will be harmed, and they will be returned to the wild, whatever that is for woodlice. Almost anywhere dark and damp I should think.'

'That came out of a discussion on why living things were motivated to move at all,' said June, one of the students who had been listening. 'Of course the obvious answer was food searching, then finding a mate. Wasn't it you, Dave,' she said, tapping the shoulder of someone who had also been interested in what Peter was telling Julie, 'who suggested that newness could be important for its own sake?'

'Yes, I was saying how eager we are for the next newspaper, or as children the weekly comic, and how advertisers never tire of using the word "new" in the commercials. You'd think it would be worn out but it never seems to be. With just three letters it certainly punches above its weight.'

'Anyway, let's go and see what Jodie and Alice have come up with,' said Peter.

They walked over to a bench, which was now surrounded by students.

'Alice, would you explain to Ms Copeland what you are planning please.'

'Well, we've got eight woodlice, each in a matchbox with a bit of rotten wood. There's a large card – brown to avoid dazzle, and there's a bicycle wheel rim as containment. Each box will be opened in turn and placed near the rim with the opening facing the centre. We'll change the card each time to avoid scent trails. Hopefully, the woodlice will leave their boxes and we'll make a copy of the routes they take.'

'The idea is to observe what happens to the movements of the woodlice given minimum stimulus,' said Jodie. 'Do they, for instance, use the earth's magnetic field to choose a direction? Out in the open, on their own, it is noticeable that they stop and start and change direction. Will they do the same when there is no stimulus? We also want to estimate how far each run is between stops.'

Alice asked the spectators to move back on the grounds that if people breathed all over them, the woodlice might modify their behaviour.

The two students began the experiment and the group watched its progress for a while before twos and threes drifted off to chat. Due to the fact that a few of the woodlice needed some encouragement to leave their boxes, some time elapsed before the experimenters cleared up and rehoused the subjects. The group reconvened and Alice promised a woodlouse report when, hopefully, the results were analysed.

Julie was delighted to be at the Science Group. The maturity and enthusiasm made a pleasant change from the classroom but then, she reflected, these were sixth formers and were there by choice. Peter seemed to get on well with them and she wondered whether things went as smoothly in the classroom. She had noticed at their first meeting his awkward movement sometimes when turning to look at something. She wondered whether only one eye gave him vision. His was a build that her ex-partner would term weedy. And look where that relationship had gone. She wouldn't rely on good looks and six packs so readily in future. Not, she told herself, that she was looking around at the moment.

The discussion began with a question from Brian. Why were the leaves at the top of holly trees smooth when those on the lower branches were prickly?

'It's an example of heterophylly,' said Peter. 'When a plant presents more than one type of leaf. But I'm not sure that the height rule is that clear cut. You can find smooth and sharp leaves on the same bough, which may support one theory that older leaves become smooth. Holly leaves have about a three-year life. Other ideas have been suggested. One involves epigenetic change while another involves the history of an individual tree, whether and how it had been trimmed.'

'I was wondering if some grafting experiments might help. Though I expect that's all been done,' said Brian.

'Brilliant idea. It doesn't matter if an experiment has been carried out. It's always worth repeating it. You might get a different result,' said Peter.

A girl called Marion volunteered to speak next. She wanted to tell the group about a simple experiment she had read about recently – one she thought might be possible for the Science Group.

'It involved about fifty plants in pots – the sort that can react quickly, like venus fly traps. Each pot was dropped a short distance and at first the plants reacted vigorously. This was repeated daily for a week and by the last drop the plants ignored that impact. As if they remembered and didn't feel threatened. The scientist presented the results to a symposium and was mildly ridiculed. I think that was a shame.'

'It certainly was,' said Peter, 'and it seems the sort of test that could be easily repeated. Perhaps we could try it.'

Peter looked around the group expectantly but no one was immediately ready, so he reminded them of Rowan Selwood's visit for the following Thursday.

'As you know we won't be here but in the lecture theatre. Now, can you all find your way there?'

Some of the students looked puzzled and there were questioning looks and shrugging of shoulders.

'No, I'm not quite off the rails,' said Peter. 'Try to imagine what it would be like if you couldn't do just that. You'd have to follow a map or, worse, ask the way. Well there are many people who have this deficiency. They may not be able to find their way around a town that they've lived in for years. Even the way home from the pub. And not always due to intoxication.'

'Is it a kind of dyslexia?' a girl called Jane asked.

'It may be related in some way,' said Peter. 'But since Selwood's ideas about memory are so striking, perhaps he may have some thoughts. There's what seems to be a similar thing that prevents some people from recognising faces. There again it can be extreme – not recognising their own children for example.'

There were a few exclamations of surprise or possibly disbelief, leading Peter to think that the group could take this subject further, though it was clear that a few of the students were familiar with the cases he had described.

One of the group, Paul, who so far hadn't spoken, put his hand up. He began to describe how reading Selwood's book had, a few weeks ago, prompted a memory of a dream he'd experienced when very young.

'Not really a dream; it didn't have a story or anything. Just looking down what might have been an avenue of trees. At the end, in sort of a mist, there was a propeller going round and I had the idea of a low drone. I got this same thing many times but it faded away as I grew up. I suppose it's just the memory of a memory now, but I do recall a feeling of anxiety whenever it happened.'

While Paul was speaking Peter noticed that Julie, standing next to him, was concentrating hard on what was being said. She was on his sighted side and, glancing, he saw there was a slight frown on her face.

Paul was continuing. 'A few years ago my mum and I were going through a box of old family history. There was a photo of a man in RAF uniform standing in a field with a powerful looking Alsatian. My mum told me that he was the brother of my great grandfather and that he'd been killed in an air accident in 1942. Anyway, after reading the book, I started thinking about memories drifting around in weird fields and wondered if my dreams could have been connected to my long ago relative.'

He paused and just at that moment, to Peter's surprise, Julie held onto his arm as if she needed support. Although this was extraordinary to Peter, Julie seemed unaware and remained focused on Paul's story. He was relating how he and his mother had begun researching his distant relative's accident and had found that it had occurred only twelve miles away on the outskirts of Cheltenham; amazingly local. It could have happened anywhere in Britain.

'It was a mid-air collision and I'm trying to find out more about it. Anyway I'd like to visit the place sometime and hoped one or two people from this group would come.'

'That might be an interesting outing. It certainly sounds intriguing,' said Peter. 'Anyway, time's up so goodbye and thanks for coming. Don't forget next week. I would bet you've a few questions lined up.'

Julie had released his arm and was laughing in the low quiet way she had, which Peter had begun to find quite attractive.

'I'm sorry if I alarmed you. I wasn't thinking.'

Peter smiled. But was that a faint twinge of disappointment at her disclaimer, he wondered?

'That's OK. I hope nothing was wrong.'

'No. That account Paul was giving resonated with me unexpectedly.'

They walked in silence down the stairs and followed the students along the corridor to the main door. Julie was frowning again.

'I really was quite startled just then,' said Julie, pausing just outside the door.

'Clearly. Do you want to talk about it?'

'Maybe. What do you do at weekends?'

Peter, taken by surprise, was momentarily at a loss.

'Well, mostly running,' he finally replied.

'Oh, I should have guessed. You've the build for it. I bet you do marathons and things.'

'A few. But I love running through the countryside round here. It's quite beautiful. Have you done any running at all?'

'I did a couple of those Race for Life things and the friend I did them with started to get serious and joined a club. But not me I'm afraid. Anyway, I was thinking maybe we could meet in town. Say, Saturday morning. I'll have had time to think about what got to me tonight and you could let me know a bit about Gloucester. I know you've been here years. Hope you don't mind me asking.'

Peter wondered how she'd found out how long he'd been around and realised that he was being a bit slow. Julie was waiting inquiringly.

'You can let me know tomorrow if you like. Is there anyone who would mind?' she asked.

'Not that I know of,' said Peter, recovering his wits.

Julie laughed.

'How about Costa then? The one in Southgate. Eleven o'clock.'

'Yup, that's fine.' Peter had planned a long slow training run for Saturday but he was not going to let go a rare and unexpected opportunity for female company. He cycled home in a warm glow, oblivious to the cutting February wind.

CHAPTER FOUR

———•———

Spring arrived suddenly. Peter slung his jacket over one shoulder, enjoying long forgotten warmth on bare arms. He was amused, as he was every year, by the number of people reluctant to leave their winter clothes at home. Julie, he saw, was not one of those. Sitting near a window in a patch of sunshine, her thigh-length cotton tunic had been chosen with a warm day in mind.

'I thought I was early,' said Peter, pointing to an empty coffee cup and a plate decorated with croissant crumbs.

Julie smiled. 'I was hungry but don't worry, I haven't finished. I'm getting a raspberry leaf tea. What can I get you?'

Peter sat down to wait, reflecting that, from her interest in the Science Group to arriving half an hour early for morning coffee, one might have to expect the unexpected from Julie.

Julie returned with their drinks, re-occupied her place in the sun and launched into an appreciation of the Science Group.

'I should mention that I got off to a bad start with science. I'll tell you about it one day, but I think your Science Group will give me a bit of optimism. It's so much what science should be. Lay people like me are told all these amazing things. Subatomic particles that exist for microseconds or the composition of distant asteroids. We sometimes get simplified explanations in the papers or on TV but those present-day wizards with their complicated equations on whiteboards, well ...' Julie shrugged her shoulders. 'Your group lets young people know that they can take part; look at things that may still be unknown.'

'I hope you're right. Pure science has become super specialised and the applications have hooked us all. I can see three people on their phones now. It's unlikely they will know much about the electronics they're using. Or care.'

'Just like me,' said Julie ruefully. 'We don't have much choice.'

Peter nodded. 'So many things have moved away from being easily understood by everyone like plumbing, cars and planes. But I think there are signs that we want to reclaim some of our world. Repair cafes for instance.'

Julie gazed out at the busy street. The subject of change had brought to mind something she'd read about that week. A group who believed that humanity should voluntarily become extinct. This was based on the conviction that human life was individually and collectively meaningless. Such views seemed to her sad and bleak in the extreme. To Julie, though not versed in science, the universe was full of wonder and mystery. She wondered whether Peter had come across the idea of a future world without humans and what he would think of it. She had been looking forward to spending time with him and hoped they would share some values. He seemed to have a calmness but at the same time always looked slightly anxious, or maybe concerned. He reminded her of the comedian Tommy Cooper but with a very different physique of course. It was said that he, Cooper, only had to appear on stage for people to laugh, so much so that he gathered an audience in the street once just by transferring Christmas shopping to his car; which annoyed him. Julie thought Peter had the same worried look.

'Have you ever thought about doing stand-up comedy, Peter?' she asked impulsively.

'That's a strange question; why did you ask that?' Peter's look became more anxious.

'Oh just a train of thought. Take no notice,' said Julie and refused to elaborate. She was annoyed with herself, since she had resolved not to be her usual grasshopper self, though she needn't have worried as Peter was finding her lively talk fascinating.

With an effort he recalled the main reason for their meeting.

'You were going to tell me what struck you about Paul's experience.'

In the months ahead Peter would look back at this simple statement as the very beginning of a long journey, the strangeness and danger of which was unimaginable on that bright cheerful morning.

'Mm, well, it was the actual type of experience that resonated with me,' began Julie.

'But the picture was entirely different. Whereas Paul saw a static scene with a revolving propeller at its centre, at the same time feeling apprehensive, mine was a stretch of water, possibly a lake. I'm standing on a slight grassy slope looking out over the water. I have a faint impression of buildings in the distance beyond the water. I have a feeling of sadness – a loss. And something I should have done.'

She looked questioningly at Peter.

'Of course, like Paul, I was very young and though the dream was repeated several times, it faded away as I grew up. Just like Paul's. So I'm left with just the memories rather than the feelings. But now I think about it, these feelings were remarkably adult for a young child.'

Julie waited for a response but Peter was gently tapping a rhythm of his own on the table and gazing out of the window.

'I'm fascinated by all dream experiences,' he said finally, 'but what you and Paul describe is a new category for me.'

'Oh, but what categories do you have then?' asked Julie.

'Well there are the anxiety dreams. I've asked other runners if they get these. I certainly do. You turn up for a race after it's started or you take a wrong turn. Mind you that happens in real life too but that doesn't feel dreamlike; just bloody annoying. Then there's coming up to exams and you realise you've done no work in the subjects.'

Julie nodded, laughing. 'Yes, I've had those, they're awful.'

'Then there are dreams that seem to predict a future happening. Not a racehorse winner or suchlike but something which you experience, perhaps next day – often something trivial.'

Julie was thoughtful. 'I think I've had those but, as you say, so trivial, like finding a coin on the pavement. But unless you record your dreams you can't be sure your mind isn't playing tricks by inventing a dream memory. Or it's all down to chance.'

'There's a book called *An Experiment with Time* that records an attempt to get over the first objection', said Peter. 'The author got eight people to record their dreams and also experiences that might relate to them. There were some striking results but what you might call proof is elusive.'

'Any other types?'

'I have very occasionally thought a dream was of something that happened to another person. I once dreamed I was trying to make a phone call from a public booth in Chicago. Me! Who's never even been to America!'

'I hope you got through,' laughed Julie. 'But seriously, if such things happen couldn't mine and Paul's thing be an example of the last type? Seeing through someone else's eyes but maybe from a long time ago.'

'It would be great to do some work on these possibilities but we have to be careful in the Science Group. Anything to do with the mind can lead to trouble with students or parents, especially anything to do with what they might call paranormal.'

'Pity.' Julie jumped to her feet. 'Meanwhile, let's get out on the streets. I ordered a tour of the city, remember.'

CHAPTER FIVE

———•———

They walked up to what is known as the Cross.

'This was said to be the busiest crossroads in England before the first Severn Bridge was built. There used to be a police constable on point duty at busy times.'

Julie stood at the centre of the Cross. 'Right here I suppose.'

She turned to face each exit in turn, taking in the varied views each offered.

'Imagine. All those old-fashioned cars — not old fashioned then of course — criss-crossing. Off to Wales or northbound. Open Rileys, Ford Populars. Perhaps the policeman shouting at any driver who'd not seen him. Now it's so calm. Just people and market stalls.'

They began strolling down Westgate Street. Julie darted to the side to read a plaque.

Peter knew that the plaque marked the site of a bank owned by a man said to have been the inspiration for Dickens' Scrooge.

'That's amazing,' exclaimed Julie. 'I can just imagine the Christmas ghosts drifting up this street and through the door.' She began laughing as the images developed in her mind. 'And Scrooge rushing out into the street on Christmas morning, maybe in his night clothes, shouting and giving away money.'

'Sadly he probably wasn't visited because he died a very wealthy man,' said Peter.

'Bet he was miserable then. Oh well, if he really was the model for Ebeneezer Scrooge then that was his gift to the world.'

Resuming their walk, Peter pointed out the squares and rectangles formed by different coloured paving stones.

'Those shapes mark out where buildings once stood.'

'Really! So this would have been two narrow streets where now there is this wide one? And they'd have been ankle deep in horse shit, plus people emptying chamber pots from windows.'

'So they say. Just round the corner there's a lane off Northgate where they overdid the narrowness. One day an ox got stuck and they had to slaughter and butcher it on the spot.'

'So glad you told me that. I'm a vegetarian you know,' chuckled Julie.

Peter turned and drew Julie's attention to an ancient timber-framed building – a survivor from Elizabethan times. He walked over to the doorway of one of the empty shops that made up the ground floor and tapped on the glass. The door opened and a tall lean man appeared, greeting Peter warmly. While they were speaking, Peter beckoned Julie over.

'Julie, this is Obuya, a running friend. Obuya, this is Julie, the colleague I told you about. I asked Obuya yesterday if we could go up to the first floor of this building. It's very atmospheric. He's allowing us to go up as long as we're really careful.'

'You'll see why when you get there,' said Obuya.

Obuya was fitting out the shop and they had to go round several obstacles to reach a dilapidated wooden door in a side wall. Behind it rose a wooden staircase, which gave a series of creaks as they ascended. At the top Julie looked round in amazement. Angled corridors led in different directions each displaying old doors on which were painted numbers. From where they stood they could see into a bathroom which housed bath, sink and toilet bowl, all very grubby and stained. They made their way slowly down the corridor, which was parallel to Westgate, noting the various gradients of the floor that indicated that the building had been added to in a random way. The smells of age and damp were pervasive.

'I'm guessing this has been some kind of hotel, and not a five star one,' said Julie.

'That's right,' said Peter. 'Way back it was an inn with accommodation for pilgrims visiting the cathedral.'

Julie went into one of the open rooms and looked out at the busy street below.

'It's like another world in here.'

She joined Peter in the centre of the room and they looked around at the peeling wallpaper and ubiquitous brown paint.

'You could let your imagination have a ball thinking of things that have gone on in this place over hundreds of years. It feels quite sleazy,' said Julie.

They went down and said goodbye and thanks to Obuya. It felt odd to be out on the street again, so they stood looking up at the black and white frontage for a few minutes.

'You'd never guess what was behind those windows. Thanks for that, Peter. It was a lovely surprise. If strange.'

They carried on wandering up and down the other roads of the Cross, taking in some of the back alleys sleeping in forgotten history.

'I get a real sense of age in this city,' said Peter. 'I think its history goes way back beyond Roman times, since this was the first place to easily cross the Severn.'

'All those people; hundreds of generations walking about hand in hand.'

Julie suddenly slipped her hand into Peter's.

'Continuity,' she said archly.

Taken by surprise, though pleasantly, Peter tried to remember what else he'd intended to show Julie but was saved by a voice from behind them.

'Yes, it's about time someone took him in hand.'

April Roberts, one of the two music teachers at their school, caught up, having clearly noticed Julie's manoeuvre.

'He needs someone to take his mind off his endless running.'

'Oh, but we're old friends,' said Julie. 'We've known each other for weeks.'

April gave them both what she imagined was a shrewd look.

'Anyway, I'm glad to have met you, Julie. I wanted to ask you what you thought of the new music.'

'Good selection. I like the Walton. Have we done it before?'

'Oh yes, it's got to be part of our repertoire. He was Duke of Gloucester after all. Richard Third,' she added for Peter's benefit.

'Right, his coat of arms is on the tower by the Cross. But what's the music?' Peter asked warily, knowing how ignorant he was in music matters.

'It's by William Walton,' said Julie. 'Prelude to the Richard Third Suite composed originally for the film with Olivier as the king. You can hear it on YouTube.'

'I remember seeing the film. Black and white classic. Olivier somehow gets me on Richard's side.'

'I agree, but before we start discussing films we've seen I'll do a quick fade. Good luck with the Tewkesbury race. I've got a couple of quid riding on it.' April swung round and headed for the cathedral.

'Thanks,' Peter called after her, then turned to Julie. 'I didn't realise you were a musician. Presumably you play in the school orchestra. What do you play?'

'Violin. It's a lot of fun and quite a challenge to keep up with some of the students. Already on grades seven and eight! And I didn't know you had a race next week. Or that bets were laid.'

'It's not serious gambling – bit of a joke really – small group, mainly runners, and I can't remember who started the betting. It's the Tewkesbury Half Marathon. Lots of runners from all over because it's a flat course. Obsessions with personal best times. Mad fools.'

'Not you, naturally,' joked Julie. 'I've just had a thought. Could I come and watch? Be your support and transport team. I'd be good at that.'

Peter wondered how he could politely turn down her offer. He couldn't accept it straight away without checking with Mike. The last things you want on race day are delay or confusion, which seem to increase unreasonably every time an extra person gets involved in anything.

'That's a kind offer. I'll have to check with my housemate. We often go together and I can't be sure he'll appreciate the help. He's a bit fussy. But won't you get bored hanging around during the race?'

'Of course not. I never get bored. I'm not sure I even know what it feels like! I'm not bored now, am I? Worse, am I boring?'

'You certainly are not boring, but I might bore you now with a lecture about bells.'

Julie yawned, then laughed as Peter's face became slightly more anxious. 'Go on then; bells.'

'Hundreds were made here just up by the museum. Bell Lane, of all places. And the best non-boring bit is that they devised a method of tuning here which didn't annoy the neighbours. Instead of bashing them to chip bits off, they turned them on a lathe. The bell in the cathedral that strikes the hour weighs three tonnes. That's bells finished.'

They pottered about until lunch time, when they bought spicy wraps. Several of their students passed the bench they sat on.

'We shall be talked about,' said Julie. 'Do you mind?'

'Not in the slightest,' replied Peter and they laughed at the absurd conversation; nevertheless, for the first time they exchanged a look that

21

caused both to wonder about the possibilities their friendship might offer.

'Are you really a vegetarian? asked Peter.

'Yes, and I'm aiming at going non-dairy one day. But I try not to force it on people. Be warned, not always successfully.' She sprang to her feet.

'I'm off now. Thanks for the morning. See you in school.'

She gave Peter a smile and quick kiss on the cheek and was gone, leaving Peter breathless.

CHAPTER SIX

Peter had to arrange a stand-in for his last lesson on Thursday in order to meet Professor Selwood at the railway station. He wasn't completely confident about recognising his visitor, so resorted to standing on the platform holding a name card. Although this felt odd, Peter was reassured when Professor Selwood greeted him good-humouredly.

The lecture theatre was full and Peter noted that the staff presence contained elements both sympathetic and otherwise to the Science Group. Perhaps some public discussion of the difference would be a good thing, but he would make sure that it didn't take up too much time. There was a pleasurable moment when Peter saw Julie in the back row. He hadn't seen her since their Saturday morning stroll despite staying vigilant. It had been quite a while since he'd experienced any romance in his life, but he didn't want to be an idiot for mistaking Julie's friendliness for anything more than that. On the other hand he would hate to miss out on the possibility of a relationship with someone he already found very attractive.

Putting aside his personal thoughts, Peter gave a short introduction and settled with his notebook as the guest took over.

'I am pleased to address the Science Group,' Selwood began. His manner, Peter noted, was easy and non-patronising. 'I have been informed about some of the work going on here and if my book helped to inspire this I am also inspired by the originality of your ideas and projects. A clear demonstration that the pursuit of science does not necessarily require megabucks. What is science and its practice anyway? Perhaps a continuous search for how, what and why. The use of systematic observation, measurement and the formulation, testing and modifying of hypotheses. Along the way there have been false paths. Deliberate frauds have been committed for power or money. Results have been modified to obtain or sustain research grants. Misleading too, have been periodic claims that there is little of importance left to discover. Well, in a universe as wonderful and complex as ours, this has so far been untrue. But, if we think back a bit, there was a time when reality did seem mechanistic and predictable. So a rift between the material and the spiritual was inevitable. But I believe that the searches for material and spiritual truths can be unified.

'As we know, to be valid, experimental results have to be repeatable given the same conditions. However, in some types of research, particularly to do with our minds and the way we think, we may not be aware of all the experimental conditions. They may involve emotions, personal agendas or moods which may not be quantifiable. This could lower the significance of results.

'One hypothesis I'm particularly interested in is that nature is structured by morphic resonance. If we assume that morphic fields exist, it could be that they shape the development of plants and animals and influence behavioural, perceptual and social phenomena. Of course, electro-magnetic and gravitational fields are easier to comprehend and a materialist scientist might well deny the existence of morphic fields rather than consider that they may have subtle, less obvious roles.

'One way in which they may work lies in the forming of habits. You may be interested in trying this out. Think about a regular routine you have, brushing your teeth or showering for instance. It's possible you can go through it without thinking, perhaps thinking of something quite different. Suppose morphic resonance uses past events to strengthen the habit. Is it difficult to make a change? If so, does the change become easier until it becomes as automatic as the original. I wonder whether birds follow repetitive algorithms when nest building. It's interesting that nests are species specific, say in shape, in the same way that we can identify a tree by its general shape though it may differ in detail.

'The hypothesis of morphic resonance is not open to easy proof but there is evidence that the production of some new crystals, difficult at first, becomes easier with time and repetition. Physical skills seem to become easier to learn for populations of animals or humans once they have been achieved by an individual.

'I suggest that memory is the tuning in to our past by morphic resonance and so actual memories are not stored in the brain, though the brain is used to access or register a memory. I would imagine that the Science Group could come up with a number of experiments relating to memory that might give some surprises.

'Now, rather than go over the contents of my book, I think the most profitable use of this session would be to discuss some of the many questions I'm sure you have. Perhaps you will chair the meeting, Mr Joy.'

'Right,' said Peter briskly. 'I've got numbered slips here so please raise your hand if you have a question.'

About fifteen hands were raised and Peter walked up the central aisle handing his tickets out randomly. Harriet, a Muslim girl, asked the first question.

'I understand from your newsletter that you attend a Christian church. What are your views on the conflict between the theories of creation and evolution?'

'An easy one to start with then,' said Selwood with a smile. 'Creationism is a belief and I suppose creationists may point to the complexity and wonder of life as proof. You could say, looking at the same wonder and complexity, that evolution itself is a design process. It's humans that are the important issue, however, because according to Islam and Christianity we did not evolve from apes. I can see no reason why any God would not use evolution to create humanity, but perhaps that idea is repugnant to creationists. Discounting a design element, random genetic mutations give rise to species variety, but it's interesting to compare that with a design that has an intelligent input as it evolves. An example would be Frank Whittle's early prototype jet engine set against a huge modern Rolls Royce equivalent with all its complexity. In nature, isn't it amazing that, from the same source, we end up with flea, octopus and giraffe. But it takes time. A long time. Imagine standing at a bus stop for an hour. You think that's a long time. Now a year, then a thousand years. Then you have to do that thousand a thousand times and you get to a million. And, if we subscribe to the evolutionary theory, life has been through hundreds of those millions. Hard to imagine.

'I try not to lose my sense of wonder at what has come to exist by whatever means. If I watch a time-lapse film showing the transformation of a dandelion flower into a seed head, I am full of admiration for the process that led to this result. And the seed head itself; what a design! No wonder it's so successful.

'Returning to morphic resonance. If it exists it will no doubt show some light on how we all got here. Book me in ten years.'

'We will,' laughed Peter. 'Next question please.'

The next question was from Elaine: 'Do you think that the differences between humans and other animals and plants are seen to be less than they used to be?'

'Definitely, yes. Research has destroyed our smug feelings of superiority by showing the huge amounts of DNA we share with not just mammals, but also insects and other creatures. Of course we're still the only ones clever enough to destroy all life on earth.

'With the proliferation of cameras, more animal behaviour can be studied, and we might find surprising similarities to our own. Watching is not necessarily understanding, though. Look up at the sky and you will see individual birds or pairs or groups criss-crossing the country. I often wonder where they have come from, where they are going and why. Look down on any town and you might ask the same questions. I was told that one of your projects touched on why life is motivated to move at all. Curiosity could be studied in its own right, I should think.'

Daniel was next in order. His was a well-off family and he was generally regarded as posh. The only reason he had not gone to a public school was his parents' strong support for the comprehensive system. He'd had no problem with that and had enjoyed his time at Elmbridge. He was popular in spite of, or perhaps because of, his self-conferred role as class wit.

'I note from your previous answer that we might be curious about curiosity.' His style if not his words drew smiles. Peter easily imagined Daniel as a future guest speaker at a Rotary Club dinner or perhaps even as a member of Parliament.

'I am aware that some members of staff at this school have reservations about the Science Group. There is a view that we students should keep our noses to the curriculum grindstone and not go chasing what might, with respect, seem like way-out ideas. What are your thoughts on that?'

Peter noted a few heads at the back turning – some exchanged glances. He had been worried about this issue coming up but hadn't expected a student to broach it. Trust Daniel, he thought. Selwood seemed not to be ruffled. He was, of course, used to opposition. He thought for a moment.

'What you are studying at Elmbridge will be foundations and you would do well to keep at the grindstone, though your work should be enjoyable rather than onerous. You will need the theoretical and practical knowledge if you wish to open up science to those way-out possibilities. You will probably know that near here Edward Jenner formalised a procedure using pus from cowpox blisters to inoculate against the then deadly disease of smallpox. This was regarded with great suspicion at the time.'

'The Jenner Museum at Berkeley is worth a visit,' Peter added. 'Next question please.'

Peter was relieved and grateful that Selwood had been tactful and of course, honest. He had sometimes half-expected the group to be closed down but, so far, always had the argument that no parents had voiced reservations.

It was inevitable that the subject of memory would crop up, since Peter had seen much interest in it at the Science Group, and as Paul had a question card a question was almost certain. Paul wanted to know why, if memories existed in fields, those fields could not be detected and measured in the normal way.

'It may be that if morphic resonance occurs, it is a personal event linked to a person's specific past and not be amenable to current technology. Or perhaps the whole thing goes beyond our mechanistic thinking. The subject of memory is absorbing and it may be worth researching the extremes, the rarities. People who are deficient in a particular way or, on the other hand, those who can remember every day of their lives after a certain date. How do memories link with dreams? How much can brain-scanning tell us? Although it has always been believed that memories are stored in the brain, no actual traces have ever been found.'

Paul raised his hand, clearly wanting to continue his question. Peter nodded assent.

'Surely memory is a component of consciousness. We have to remember from moment to moment what the previous moment was like. To detect movement, for instance, or to understand a simple spoken sentence.'

'That's an interesting thought,' said Selwood. 'It occurs to me that when a situation changes abruptly the state of consciousness of a person can also change. A sudden accident can bring on a state we may call shock. I'd be interested to hear of any related experiments you could devise.'

Paul seemed satisfied with the reply. Peter wondered if he was trying to make connections with his repetitive dream experience.

The session ended with a few questions about Selwood's book and advice on various careers in science. Selwood spoke for some time about his own career, after which Peter brought the evening to a close with sincere thanks to their visitor for his time.

CHAPTER SEVEN

J ulie caught up with Peter and Selwood in the school car park.

'I really enjoyed that meeting. Can I buy you both a drink?'

Peter was taken aback; something he was getting used to where Julie was concerned. He looked at his watch.

'There's a pub by the station. We'll have time for a quick one. How about it, Professor?'

'Yes, but not if you're going to call me that. I think we can resort to first names now, OK?'

'Fine, well this is Julie. A colleague.'

'Not science I'm afraid – languages.'

'We'll let you in if you're buying,' said Peter.

The pub had a mid-week quietness and their guest was glad to end his visit socially in a place where conversation was possible. Meeting the group of young people with an interest in expanding scientific views had been rewarding and the three spent some time evaluating the visit and the Science Group in general.

'Actually, Julie,' said Selwood after a pause in the conversation, 'as a language teacher who is also interested in science, you might like to consider investigating bird communication. I've heard of some interesting things going on in that field. Slowing down recordings and such like.'

Julie looked startled for a moment.

'What a brilliant idea. I'd never considered non-human language. Thank you for suggesting it. Perhaps one or two students at the Science Group might be interested.'

Peter looked positive and nodded.

'Well, with that I'll take my leave. I know my train's not due for twenty minutes but for some reason I like the ambience of stations. Many thanks again for the invitation.'

'Was it something we said?' laughed Julie as the door closed behind their visitor.

'Hope not, maybe waiting on platforms helps him think. There's that sense of expectancy,' said Peter.

'Whatever. Anyway, back to our own low-level lives. I wanted to tell you that I'm going with Paul and his mum to the crash site a week on Saturday.'

'Crash site?'

'Yes, you remember his account at the Science Group of dreams he had when very young, which he thinks could be aviation related. Well, whether or not they were related to his great grandfather and involving some sort of memory transfer, he still wants to make it a pilgrimage. And since it was on her side of the family his mother wants to come too. They had no idea that the accident happened near here. It seems odd but maybe things like that were affected by security during the war and afterwards they just faded away. People had enough to do getting going again in so-called peace time. Also I've been trying to recreate my own early dream experience but nothing so far. Do you think it's a good idea?'

'Just be careful. It all depends on the sort of person you are now, and I don't really know that.'

Julie smiled. 'Would you like to find out?'.

Peter, recklessly by his usual standards, replied with warmth, 'Yes, very much.'

'Good. Shall we get going and could you give me a lift home? I've left my car at school. I can walk in the morning. I often do.'

As they drove off Peter remembered that he was going to have to turn down Julie's offer of transport to the Tewkesbury Half Marathon.

'I'm really sorry about that but Mike wasn't keen. He gets very anxious about times on race days and since he doesn't know you he didn't want to introduce more uncertainties.'

'That's OK, but I've looked up all the details so I might come along anyway to cheer. I expect boy and girlfriends do that sometimes.'

'Do you think we might qualify?'

'Maybe. We'll have to see.'

Peter pulled up as directed in front of a semi-detached house, one of a row in a quiet street near the northern ring road.

'I'm not going to invite you in for coffee. Much too busy, but you can see me to my door. Do you have an umbrella in the car?'

Peter looked up through the windscreen at the clear night sky.

'Will we need one?'

'You never know, it could rain at any minute.'

'Really! Well I'm afraid there isn't one.'

'We'll just have to pretend then. Let's get out and put it up.'

Peter was beginning to recognise Julie's bizarre humour and decided he would have to fall in with it. He got out of the car and began fumbling with the imaginary umbrella with accompanying expressions of annoyance.

'Can't work the bloody thing,' he said irritably.

'Let me have a go.' Julie leaned over and joined the charade, making sure there was hand contact.

'There we are.' Julie swung the umbrella with a flourish.

They walked up the path, laughing at their silliness. But Julie hadn't finished with the play yet.

'Hmm, it's quite a small umbrella, bit of a squeeze for two but I do believe I felt a drop of rain.'

She put an arm round Peter's waist and pulled herself close until they reached the door.

'Put that thing down for a second, please.'

Peter shook the imaginary umbrella and put it carefully down. Her kiss was gentle but sensual and Peter responded enthusiastically. She had, with her humour, set a first kiss up perfectly, their laughter combined with passion overcoming Peter's obvious shyness. There was no need for further talking and they would have parted without another word but for Julie mischievously reminding Peter about the umbrella. Thus prompted, he picked it up and, raising it above his head, marched off down the path. How true that old cliche is, he thought, about walking on air.

CHAPTER EIGHT

———•———

Julie called for Paul and his mother as arranged on Saturday morning. The weather was overcast and a light drizzle was falling. In the autumn the day would have been sombre, but now, in spring, the fresh greens and colourful blossoms gave gaiety to the town streets and country lanes. Paul was excited to be setting out on what he now regarded as a pilgrimage, though without all the wearisome walking that he'd heard was usually entailed. He had with him all the details of the accident that could be gleaned from the internet and had planned the route. After hearing about Julie's similar early-life memory he knew that she would have an interest in his planned trip. After checking that Paul's mother would be coming, Julie agreed to drive them to the site.

Sandra, Paul's mother, explained to Julie how awareness of the crash and the loss of Daniel had faded through the decades and that there was no one left alive who had known him.

'This is a bit like one of those TV programmes. You know, like "Who Do You Think You Are?"' said Sandra.

'Yes, and you know,' replied Julie, 'it makes me realise how little awareness I have of my own past family beyond my grandparents. I suppose such things aren't important when you're young – much too busy growing up and getting on with the present. The past seems almost like some old fossil, especially now with technology so far ahead of what was around just fifty years ago.'

'I wonder if peer pressures have increased,' said Paul. 'For us it started when we were quite young and escalated. I think most six-year-olds have phones now. Imagine what your grandparents would have thought of that!'

They headed away from Cheltenham towards Bishop's Cleeve and were soon approaching the last stage of their journey along small country roads. Paul concentrated on his map and instructions, which he relayed to Julie, soon guiding them to a T-junction of lanes.

'I think this is it.' Julie pulled over and stopped the car. The wipers on intermittent were the only sound as they looked out over the silent fields. Paul got out and walked to the corner, followed by Sandra and Julie. He was looking across the field held by one of the right angles of the junction.

'There. Somewhere along that boundary but some way into the field. That's where they came down.'

'Did you say someone witnessed the collision?' asked Julie.

'Yes. A postboy delivering telegrams. I wonder if any were those missing in action ones. Ironic really that he should have been there.'

Paul described what the postboy had seen: the monoplane diving towards the fragile Tiger Moth, which had suddenly started to climb.

'I suppose the Tiger Moth wasn't expected to change its flight,' ended Paul.

The three stood looking at the field, each with their own thoughts and images. Julie was thinking that the morning back in 1942 had probably been as peaceful as this one. There would have been the faintest drone of approaching aircraft in the distance, getting louder until the sound filled the countryside. Then that dreadful grinding crunch that shouldn't have happened.

Eventually Paul spoke. 'That may be the farmhouse over there. I'd like to go over to see if there's any information still around. Probably not.' But there he was wrong.

The lanes were too narrow to park the car, so they drove the short distance to the farmhouse and stopped just inside the entrance. Sandra was nervous.

'Whenever I visit a farm, I don't know; I always feel I'm trespassing and that a fierce dog will appear or someone with a shotgun. Silly isn't it?'

'We'll look after you,' said Paul with a smile as they set off towards the front door of the house.

The appearance of two women and a young man was clearly a surprise to the man answering the door.

'We're sorry to disturb you ...' began Julie.

'I know. You've broken down – no, not so drastic, you've run out of fuel,' said the man with a grin as he eyed their parked car.

'Neither. But something much more unlikely. We're trying to find out more about the air accident that happened here in 1942. Do you know about that event?' asked Julie.

The man stared at them for a few seconds.

'I'm sorry, how rude of me. I am just so amazed. Yes I know about the accident. I was sort of brought up on the legend. But why are you looking into it now?'

'One of the pilot trainers was my great grandfather.' Paul got the revelation in before his companions.

'Wow. Fantastic. Well come in. Tea or coffee? I'm Joe by the way.'

'I'm Paul, this is my mother Sandra, and this is Miss Copeland.'

'Julie,' added Julie.

'A teacher from my school.'

They sat in a large room steeped in the feeling of perhaps two centuries of farm living. Generations of this family had occupied the house through good times and bad, experiencing joy and tragedy along the way. The heavy old furniture with its accompanying scent of beeswax spoke quietly of history. The modern world made itself felt in the form of a small music system and a wide television screen. Joe disappeared for a few minutes then brought in the teas and coffees they had requested.

'Well, this is really interesting, but it's my father who'll be most struck by it. He was a young boy when it happened but it was a big event in his life. I hope you can wait for him. He's just gone over to Cheltenham with my wife'.

They assured him that there was no great hurry and that they would really like to meet his father. Joe took them round the house, some of which dated from the seventeenth century. He told them that the farm kept around a hundred sheep currently but that most of the fields were arable, the land being flat and quite fertile.

Eventually they heard a Land Rover of the modern kind pull into the yard and after some audible fussing an elderly man entered the room, followed by his daughter-in-law. Joe's father made his way over, with several sideways glances towards the visitors, to what was clearly his armchair, which Joe had tactfully kept empty. When he was settled Joe introduced Paul and his companions and explained why they had come. You could imagine that nothing would surprise the old man after his many years of family life and the hard knocks of farming. Evidently this was an exception.

'Well bless my soul,' was his reaction, repeated several times. He gave Paul a long thoughtful look and it was left to Joe to start the conversation about the crash, although it was Eric, Joe's father, who contributed most since he had been on the scene and Paul had many questions ready for him. When these ran out the discussion lagged, but Eric suddenly became conspiratorial.

'You have really amazed me today,' he said, addressing Paul. 'But now I have a surprise for you, young man. Margaret, you know what I'm after and you know where to find them. Could you run and fetch that box?'

Joe's wife, who had been unobtrusively following the discussion, left the room and could be heard ascending the old wooden staircase. She returned with a box file which Eric opened and began rummaging through, soon extracting a battered envelope. From this he withdrew what looked like a few postcards, which he examined then handed to Paul.

'There you are. No one's looked at those for decades.'

Paul took the cards and realised they were photographs, slightly yellowed with age. After a glance he gasped.

'Is that it – the wreckage?'

'That's it, the day after.'

For Paul, this was hard to take in. Never had he hoped to see such images. The photographs showed the wreckage of both aircraft in the field, the Tiger Moth remains in the foreground with the monoplane further from the hedge in the distance. There were four cards and they were passed around in silence.

'Thank you so much,' said Paul when he had seen them all. 'But how did these get taken?'

'Ah, well it happened that one of the land girls – you know about them perhaps?' Paul nodded. 'One of them had a Brownie Box camera and luckily there was film in it. But getting these pictures was not straightforward. She and my father worried that the pictures might be censored if they took the film to a chemist to be developed. That was the usual way in those days. Not like now eh, with your cameras holding hundreds of images? Anyway, one of the girls had a boyfriend who knew someone who had the equipment to develop the film so off it went. What a fuss, but we got these back about a month later and here they've waited all this time for you. Of course all the wreckage had long gone so these pictures were the only evidence the accident had ever happened. I was five and one of the land girls took me over the field to see the remains before they were cleared. Can't remember her name but I expect there's a record in that file.'

35

'What else happened afterwards?' Julie asked.

'Not a lot really. I think by that time in the war people had a different attitude to events. So many disasters and deaths. A building in central London if it burned and collapsed now would be a major news story. But during the blitz that happened to hundreds of buildings. Anyway, a man from the Air Ministry arrived and took statements, including from the telegraph boy, who was the only eye witness. Some RAF ground crew cleared the wrecks. Then a couple of years later – it was still wartime – the wife of one of the pilots came. Sort of a pilgrimage I suppose. She had her young son with her'.

'Which pilot, do you know?'

'Yes. It was the senior pilot in the Moth – Daniel his name was'.

Sandra gasped. 'That would be my father with his mother, my grandmother. Would they have come in here then, to this room?'

'Yes indeed. My parents made them very welcome. They stayed the night and I was able to play with your dad and show him some of the machinery. But it was an emotional visit for your grandmother. She was in tears a couple of times. Such an unnecessary accident, and not even near the actual war. Is your dad still alive?'

'Sadly no. Pity, that could have been quite a reunion.'

Sandra looked around the room in awe.

'It's been truly amazing. We had no idea we could be brought so close to something so distant. Thank you so much.'

'Pretty amazing for me too,' said Eric. 'And you, Paul, if I just take some copies, can keep those snaps. They belong more with you than with us.'

This was so much more than Paul had expected and he found it difficult to show the extent of his appreciation. All three in the end expressed their sincere gratitude, however, and, the copies having been made, they drove out of the farm gates, changed people in different degrees.

Each of them had good reason to ponder the visit and the car was silent for the first miles home. Julie was wondering yet again whether Paul's early dreams were of the same type as her own and whether they really meant anything at all.

'Do you think you were somehow called to visit the location – somehow a destiny for you?' she eventually got round to asking.

'It's a wonderfully dramatic thought,' replied Paul. 'But no, I don't think so. Although when you think about it I was pretty keen to see the site.'

Julie felt some disappointment, though she knew that to be unreasonable. The idea of memories from the past had stirred her and the thought that her childhood dreams could actually mean something had, she had to admit, excited her. In particular, would they explain her lifelong feeling of something incomplete? Closure was the word everyone bandied around now. But didn't everyone have such feelings to some extent? There need be no mystery. Yet what about the sad feelings, the feeling of loss? Where did they come from?

Tiring of questions with no real answers, she changed the subject by announcing that she intended to support Peter in his race next weekend.

'Whoay,' exclaimed Paul. 'Have you ever seen Mr Joy run?'

'I never have yet.'

'Ha ha.'

'What do you mean ha ha?'

'You'll see.'

'Paul!'

But Paul refused to explain and left Julie to wonder.

CHAPTER NINE

Julie wakes up. Something has happened but she has no idea what it could be. There is a familiar sense of loss. She looks round the room but nothing is out of place. Bounce, her pet rabbit, has died, but that was years ago, decades. Gradually the feeling that is nudging her mind comes into focus and recognition strikes with long-forgotten sorrow. She knows in an instant that these are the memories from childhood. She has experienced the dream that had faded to nothing as the years passed. Still there, the stretch of water, the grass slope and a town skyline beyond.

But what was this sadness? Sadness so familiar yet seemingly not tied to any reality. She thought again of her rabbit, whose death had been her most intense experience of painful bereavement. The death of her father had led to quite different feelings, amongst which was the guilt that had increased over the years. This was more subtle. Like a faint scent, familiar but not identifiable and somehow inviting, like a ghost beckoning.

Julie relaxed on her bed and tried to recapture the scene from her sleep. Was this visitation brought on by going with Paul to the crash site? But Paul had been quite down to earth about it all. At least he had been so far. But what had Paul's family and early dream to do with these images of hers?

She remembered what Rowan Selwood had said about so-called paranormal or psychic phenomena. That perhaps conditions had to be a certain way and that we may not know what these were.

Her alarm clock, set for waking on a school day, put an end to her speculations. She shook off the dream and the feelings it had brought on and went through her normal morning routine. In the car she thought about the problems she had with some of her students. She was good at introducing imaginative topics to get bored classes interested, though not when the inspectors were around.

Imagination. What was it? The Science Group had aroused her interest in so many things. Surely animals were imaginative. How else would squirrels solve problems set by experimenters using food as incentive unless they were able to picture solutions and evaluate them? But could imagination get you into trouble? She certainly did not want to ascribe importance to her dreams if they were of no significance. Perhaps the night's happening would never be repeated. Put aside now, it need never trouble her again. Curiosity, huh, she thought, who needs it?

By the time she reached school the shadows of the night had vanished. She didn't mention them to Peter when they met briefly in the staff room. Neither did she remind him that she was coming to see his race, being almost sure he hadn't taken her seriously about that particular plan. By the end of the school day Julie had decided that if the dream image appeared again she would start looking for clues on the internet.

CHAPTER TEN

There was plenty of room on the two parking fields, even though several hundred cars had already arrived. Julie soon realised that this event was very different from the races in the park she had taken part in. There were no hippos or pirates, not even a parrot. Runners of all sizes and ethnicities were determinedly warming up, a colourful mobile patchwork across and around the fields. Some serious competitors were already out on the nearby roads, occasionally sprinting short distances then jogging to recover.

There was no sign of Peter, which surprised her. She thought she would find him easily and she was keen to find out what Paul had meant – 'You'll see,' he had said. What could be the mystery? Fancy dress she could now rule out, unless Peter was the only one, and how embarrassing that would be. Did he hop all the way to raise money? She wandered round the field, taking in the small marquees for refreshments or luggage, or in one case pre- and post-race massage. The PA system boomed jovially, reading messages from friends and families and giving details of the race and its history.

'That's great. You've come to give me a cheer.'

Julie turned to see her former fellow fun-runner. They laughed with a hug and Julie explained why she was there. Scanning the site as she talked, she spotted Peter near the start area.

'Oh, there he is, that's a relief. I was starting to think he hadn't turned up.'

'Which is he?'

'The one with the blue vest; there.'

Julie started to run towards Peter but Penny called to stop her.

'Better see him at the end, Julie. He'll be focusing on the start now and probably won't want to be distracted. Not like me, he's an elite runner you know.'

'No, I didn't know actually. Wow, so I'd better take your advice. What's his time likely to be then?'

'Oh, around sixty-five, seventy minutes.'

Julie did a quick sum.

'Bloody hell, Penny, that's around five-minute mileing. I had no idea.'

'That's the sort of thing they do. Not plodding along for an hour and forty – my style.'

'That sounds all right to me.' Julie looked her friend over. 'I'm glad you kept on with the running. You look well on it.'

'How about you?'

'I suppose I could have another try at it. I need to do something but I won't be jogging along with him I guess.'

'He's getting on towards world class. Oh, I have to be nosy now … are you …?'

Julie interrupted. 'It's early days but it's a possibility.'

'Great. Good luck then. I might see you later if you haven't gone home by then! I'm off for a pre-race pee. I can see the queues are getting longer.'

'I promise to cheer you in. Run well.'

Penny trotted off towards the mass of runners, leaving Julie to keep a low profile until a klaxon sent them on their way. The fields suddenly felt quiet and empty, though there were plenty of supporters and organisers still dotted about. The address system soon got into its stride again, relaying progress out on the course. Peter's name soon came up, along with three or four leading runners. Julie found it strange to feel associated with someone who was clearly a celebrity in the limited world of running. From being an outsider she suddenly felt involved. She tried to follow the commentary, quickly becoming strongly partisan, and felt frustrated when she heard of a 40 metre gap between her man and two leaders. Come on, Peter, she thought, willing him on. She would like to have driven out to some point on the course to give Peter a surprise, but with the speed of these leaders she'd probably miss the finish. The situation called for a calming cigarette, though after lighting up she felt more than usually guilty and even wondered whether smoking was banned in the vicinity. She was going to have to have another go at quitting.

It seemed no time before her watch showed that the race had been going for nearly an hour. The commentator was bellowing that the leaders were in the last mile. She decided to stand at the rope marking the route but about a hundred metres away from the finish line, which was marked by a huge banner stretched above the grass. She felt the excitement mounting around her as the runners appeared and there was a crescendo of noise from the spectators, some of whom were shouting for individual runners, though most just shouting. She visually confirmed what the commentary was gabbling; that Peter was in third place but there was a fourth man closing as they came pounding down the home straight. Julie was shouting at the top of her voice, though she knew no one person would be heard above the cheering of the crowd. Peter was making a huge effort to get into second place but both were overtaken by the late comer. The announcer gave Peter third place. It must have been very close, Julie thought as she made her way to the finish area. The men looked exhausted. Peter was lying on his back with one knee raised and only opened his eyes when Julie crouched next to him and whispered. He was clearly amazed and delighted to see her but beyond raising a hand in greeting made no attempt to move.

'Well done. That was truly thrilling.'

'Shouldn't have been really. Usually more spread out. Like that.' He pointed to the finish where runners were arriving with long gaps.

'Well you kept pretty quiet about that didn't you? This elite runner thing. I'm very impressed.'

'Give us a haul up then.'

Julie grasped one of the proffered hands and leaned back using her weight to drag Peter up. His weight was greater than expected. Solid muscle she supposed.

'Medals and prizes are over there,' said Peter pointing to a striped marquee. 'In about an hour if you're interested.'

'I'll try but I have to cheer my friend in first.'

After a sweaty hug they went their separate ways. This time Julie walked further along the course to hopefully make herself heard. There was a fascination in watching the runners stream by; seeing the differing running styles and the degrees of exhaustion evident. She almost forgot to look out for Penny, so interested was she in watching everyone. But at an hour and thirty-five minutes she spotted her target and willed Penny, with much vocal aid, to look her way. Penny glanced over and managed a tortured smile but was clearly intent on either reeling someone in before the finish or getting a personal best time or both. Julie went to the end of the roped pathway the runners queued along for their medals. Marvelling that all these people had just run thirteen miles, she walked down the line until she reached Penny.

'Well done. You looked impressive.'

'Yeah, I'm pleased. That was a PB – 1.37.20. Thanks for cheering me in – that was really nice. I'm straight off home for a shower and a nap. Please apologise for me and you can collect my prize! Just a joke, Julie,' seeing her puzzled look. 'I haven't reached those heights yet. Bye. I might see you at another race. Maybe you'll be running.'

Julie felt quite proud on Peter's behalf at the prize and medal awards. Third place was obviously considered prestigious in this small pond, especially when the first four places were all within ten seconds. She recognised the winner but took a moment to place him, then realised that he'd been introduced as a running friend of Peter's when they'd visited the old inn in Gloucester. He had been working on the downstairs premises but for the life of her she couldn't remember his name.

'Obuya,' said Peter. 'He's Kenyan. You get loads of brilliant runners from there. You sometimes hear stories of them running six miles to school and back every day. Barefooted most likely.'

'Well, you weren't far behind him. I had no idea I was getting such a well-regarded boyfriend.' She had heard various comments in the award marquee, including something about Olympics.

Peter smiled modestly. 'How about a celebration then? I could bring round a bottle or two of Prosecco tonight.'

'Two? We have to work tomorrow. With that in mind, yes. If you've got the energy.'

'Don't worry about that. A run like that keeps me going for days.'

Julie hoped there was some promise in this claim. She was pleased that Peter was taking the initiative. The power she'd seen, not only Peter's but of all the fast runners, had been sensuously appealing and, as it turned out, she was not to be disappointed. A warm spring evening brought subtle new scents only experienced in spring. The understanding between them that this was the time to make love didn't need words.

Julie lay back later in a state of complete relaxation.

'Are you always that good, or do we always have to wait for a race?'

'Hopefully you'll get the chance to find out.'

'Suits me,' she said dreamily and drifted into sleep.

When the alarm clock woke her, Peter was gone, leaving a note that just said, 'Thank you. See you later.'

Great in bed, but I won't expect outstanding love letters, thought Julie, as she reluctantly got out of bed to face Monday morning. But what else do you expect from a scientist?

CHAPTER ELEVEN

– London 1860

———•———

George Yeoman and his three brothers and sister had never seriously questioned their roles and futures in the family business. They had grown up in the hustle and noise of the Covent Garden wholesale fruit and vegetable market, each learning stage by stage the different aspects of the firm. Over the years there had been various family disputes. Sometimes these concerned relationships and at other times practical or monetary matters. Victor and Queenie always allowed their children their say and so cultivated an interest which survived, even thrived on, the stresses of commerce.

Ever since a visit to the Great Exhibition in 1851, Victor had become very aware of changes taking place in Britain, both social and industrial. He tried to pass this awareness on to his children and enrolled them in private and church schools where they became numerate and literate. He and Queenie often discussed the future and how their offspring would fare.

Several years earlier, Victor had proposed that the family open a shop. The idea had seemed strange and much reflection went on as to whether it could be done. Queenie had been completely shocked at the first suggestion. After only a few minutes thought her response was not encouraging.

'I suppose you'll be wanting a small holding next, then we can do the whole lot.'

'No, too risky,' replied Victor, seemingly oblivious of the sarcasm.

'Risk. You talk about risk.'

Queenie went off muttering and wondering what had come over her husband. Many objections to the idea arose but with the four children quickly becoming not children, the advantages of expanding were promising to outweigh the problems. There was no likelihood of increasing their wholesale trade since they had pushed the extent of their Covent Garden stake to the limit. The family could of course branch out into another trade, or their offspring might take up apprenticeships. Victor, however, having conceived the idea, was keen on extending geographically with what they already knew.

The plan was never mentioned outside the family circle. Not even to the scattered outer relatives who had their own concerns. The obvious financial advantages were chewed over. The retailing of stock already purchased by the wholesaling side and the consequent sharing of risks was a positive factor. But the driving motive was to keep the family together without the overstaffing, which would occur until Victor and Queenie retired. That seemed a long way off. The two elders loved the work and the business they had built almost from scratch. They enjoyed the busy activity each morning as the suppliers arrived with their varied horse or hand-drawn carts. They had built good friendships with suppliers and customers alike and, in spite of the endless banter, which they loved, there was plenty of goodwill in their trading activities both buying and selling.

The possible location of a shop was much discussed periodically, especially at the Sunday family gathering over dinner where matters were hammered out in mostly good humour. If there was to be a Yeoman's Grocers it would have to be well away from any of their existing customers. Any hint that anyone might lose income due to the Yeoman family would spread rapidly round the closed world of Covent Garden and would do them no good at all.

Various districts were listed and George was entrusted with the task of plodding round them to look for a suitable location and, if possible, premises. He found it a novel and pleasant experience to be released from the daily routine to roam around London, a city which, like many parts of Britain he supposed, was changing and expanding rapidly. The late summer weather was conceding to autumn but the dry spell which had begun in early September was holding, making walking easy. He was thankful for the absence of mud and horse dung.

New residential building work was progressing in some parts and George had to guess what opportunities might soon exist as a result. Passing through the established centres of Camden Town and Kentish Town it was obvious that the local population was well served with basic provisions. Some of Yeoman's own customers had sold here for decades. Passing on, Holloway looked promising with no apparent vegetable outlet. George spotted a row of old cottages that were being demolished. A man in overalls was calling to two others inside, giving them instructions. George asked him why the buildings were going.

'Rotten right through, sir. Not worth anyone's trouble.'

'Who was living in them and where have they gone?'

The man shrugged.

'No idea, sir. I ride over from Edmonton each day – not from round here. Good stone in these cottages though. It'll all be re-used on the new building no doubt.'

George gathered that a new police station was to be built, combined with a magistrate's court.

'Of course it'll have water and gas supplied. And sewerage I suppose. Everywhere will be like that soon enough. Being a builder I have to move with the times. Good day to you, sir. I must get on.'

He picked up a large crowbar and disappeared inside one of the cottages.

George saw, as he continued his journey, the validity of the man's forecast. Trenches were being dug not just for new buildings but for those built forty years or more earlier. He wondered whether to try further east or even get down to South London. He took out one of the coins he'd brought and used it to decide. North or south. East or west. After several coin tosses he started off in a north-westerly direction.

His new plan was to head for Highgate, where Richard Whittington was supposed to have paused before coming to London to follow his illustrious career. He looked forward to seeing the famous view that Whittington must have enjoyed at that critical moment in his life. Perhaps when he got there something similar might happen for George, though possibly on a lesser scale. At this point an idea, which when he set out had been a mere fantasy, the faintest daydream, now presented itself as a possibility. Having let a coin decide his route, he could be absolved from responsibility. The idea was to pass by the farm belonging to one of Yeoman's suppliers and where lived the young lady he had briefly met during several of the early morning deliveries. He knew the farm was in the vicinity of Highgate and he hoped it would not be far from the main road heading north. He would have to ask directions as he drew nearer and as he progressed he felt a slight pleasant fluttering in his belly indicating an excitement that had nothing to do with his search for properties.

As it turned out George found the farm without having to enquire. Just a lucky turn off the main road, which he took to be a good omen. It was at this point that he realised the difficulty that might arise when it came to explaining his presence in the area. He was under strict orders not to divulge the family secret to anyone. After toying with various completely spurious ideas he decided he might as well go straight to the truth. If asked by anyone, then he came to call on Tillie. If Tillie herself was around he would summon up all his courage and ask her to walk out with him. Having resolved the problem he briskly covered the distance to the farm gate, his excitement mounting.

'Good day, sir. Can I help you?' Adrian Hopkins strolled across the yard towards George. Recognition dawned as he drew closer. 'Why it's young George. This is a surprise, and what are you doing out here in the wilds. I hope there's no complaint with our produce. No that can't be,' he chuckled. 'I'll wager you don't get better than ours.'

Mr Hopkins stood, arms folded, smiling at George and waiting for a response.

'No complaints whatever, sir. We're always delighted with your deliveries. As a matter of fact I'm doing a bit of a tour for some other family business but I've steered a course here with the idea of, well … wondering if I could make a better acquaintance with … well …'

'Tillie,' filled in Mr Hopkins. He was going to have to disappoint George and he felt sorry for that. He admired the Yeomans and their brood and if circumstances had been different he would have welcomed George's interest in Tillie.

'I'm very much afraid someone's beaten you to her – she's due to be wed in a month or two.'

George's face fell briefly but he recovered quickly. 'I suppose I should have expected that, sir. Such beauty would hardly remain unclaimed for long.'

'That may well be so, George, and I hope better fortune awaits you. Meanwhile come and try a cup of our old cider to drown your sorrows.' Mr Hopkins smiled sympathetically and patted George on the back. He remembered such setbacks from his own youth.

They crossed the yard to the cider barn with its barrels and presses. The cider was very dry and, George guessed, very strong. He was careful to keep the conversation on day-to-day business. Mr Hopkins was curious about George's mission but thankfully was polite enough not to make enquiries. Mrs Hopkins walked over to the barn after a while and was delighted to see George, making sure he left the farm with a hefty slice of pie and a quart of the old cider. It was a glorious autumn evening, heavy with scents of fruit and hay. It seemed a shame to have to find a bed somewhere so George settled for the south-facing side of a haystack where, with the help of pie and cider, he reviewed his progress. He was intrigued by the fact, mentioned by Mr Hopkins, that Tillie was engaged to a railway worker, a locomotive fireman to be exact. George had scant experience of the railways but was becoming aware of the changes they were bringing. People were covering distances in times previously undreamed of and George could see that food produce would soon be carried from places further afield than horse-drawn transport could manage. His planned route tomorrow would take him near two railways and he decided he would look at them with a new interest. There must be something in them to attract a girl like Tillie!

CHAPTER TWELVE

———•———

The scent of hay was confusing and for a few seconds George wondered where he was. Amazed that he should have slept so well he sat up and surveyed the surrounding countryside. The sun was on the point of rising and long patterns of bright light soon appeared across the fields. A church bell was faintly tolling, prompting George to make a move, firstly to find breakfast.

As he went over to the track he saw a man walking towards him. Since his own route lay in the same direction, George waited to greet the stranger. From what seemed to be a toolbag slung over a shoulder, George adjudged him to be a working man and, from the patched dusty clothes, down on his luck. If his clothing was in poor condition his shoes were in a worse state, clearly only held together by lengths of rope and leather. George felt keenly his own good fortune, signified by adequate clothing and footwear, but if the man bore any resentment he showed no sign of it and the two fell easily into conversation. Henry was a stonemason whose last job had ended with the completion of a church extension some time ago. He'd since found no new employment and was now on the tramp, hoping to reach Portsmouth where a new hospital was about to be built at Netley.

'Trouble is there'll be a good many others with the same idea,' he said grimly.

They were silent for a bit. Henry sat down on the grassy side of the track, no doubt glad of a rest. George reflected how fortunate his position was and on the hardness of the lives of many other men.

'And you'll be on foot all that way. Will your shoes hold out?'

'They'll have to won't they,' Henry laughed.

He looked up and pointed. George followed his gaze. Two buzzards were circling lazily in the early morning sun, calling to each other as they made their way across country.

'That's a fine way to travel, ain't it? And as the good Lord says, they toil not neither do they spin.'

'With wings like that you'd be at Portsmouth in a day. But look here, though your good fortune's yet to come, you could do with a morsel of it now. I'm after some breakfast and I hereby invite you to join me at my expense. If we can only find some.'

'I am pleased to accept your offer,' began Henry formally but with a twinkle, 'and can only hope that when this good fortune that you confidently predict arrives, we shall meet again when I shall return the favour.'

They set off in silence. Thoughts about his mission occupied George as he imagined finding the perfect location and premises for his family's venture. These daydreams kept him occupied for a mile or so, after which he began to think about railways, prompted by the fact that, as he approached Primrose Hill, steam whistles could be heard.

Railways had not yet played an active part in George's life, though it was impossible not to hear and read about their expanding networks and occasional accidents. As he approached the line that ran up from Euston Station, he felt a new interest and excitement. He knew that there was a powerful engine which hauled trains up the slope from the great terminus but as they approached he was disappointed not to see it in action. What they both were very pleased to find, however, was a stall selling food for railway workers. Many of the railway's activities were centred here, and there were facilities set up to serve the needs of the workers. While they enjoyed their bowls of pea soup and hunks of bread and dripping, George continued his thoughts, which now concerned his own position in the world. Could he in fact leave the family business and follow a new career in what were exciting times? He'd never seen the sea but couldn't imagine taking to shipboard life, and he'd always felt intimidated by the rough closed world of the docks. Neither did factories with their noise and many accidents appeal. But railways. Here was something offering great variety and there was an energy here that was driving the whole project along, through tunnels, over viaducts, searing across farmland and moors alike. He decided he would combine family business with a visit to Paddington Station as, after all, the whole of this part of London should be looked at.

George and Henry handed back their bowls and prepared to go their ways. Before they parted however, George, who could not imagine Henry's boots lasting much longer, decided to intervene.

'It's just a loan mark you,' he said with what he hoped was the same twinkle in his eye that Henry had shown earlier.

'I mind that. May you and your present search fare well.'

George watched as Henry set off, hoping the half sovereign he had given him would speed his way. He wondered how Henry had known he was on a quest but there was no answer to that. It did remind him, however, that he'd completely forgotten to visit the Whittington Stone. The sweetness of anticipating a meeting with Tillie and the bitterness of disappointment had put it from his mind. Now he really must get on with what he was supposed to be doing.

He was struck by the fact that the Primrose Hill area had commercial potential. A row of three-storey residences with space for shops had been built quite near the hill. One of the houses was clearly occupied and after brushing himself down and attempting to avoid the look of having spent the night in a haystack, he knocked at the front door. A small rosy-cheeked woman answered and George asked where he could obtain information regarding the empty properties.

'Well, my master and mistress are away today but you're in luck my lad 'cos I, being incurably inquisitive, can tell you of the law firm who are dealing with it.'

The woman, who from her jolly presence and floury apron George took to be the cook, gave him the name and whereabouts of the solicitors handling the properties. Departing with a wink, which seemed to amuse her, he left picturing her as a future customer of Yeoman's Fruit and Vegetable Shop. He knew the Regent Canal led towards Paddington and followed the waterway along several paths and lanes since the towpath itself was out of bounds to the public. Several pairs of loaded narrowboats passed as he walked along, their powerful shire horses travelling at a rate not much faster than his own walking pace. George thought of the speeds of steam locomotives and wondered how long the canals would remain profitable.

As he approached the great terminus at Paddington he saw three men in overalls, perhaps, he thought, about to start their shift. One was about his own age and the other two he judged to be in their forties. Assuming they were in fact railway workers he fell into step with them. There was a pause in their conversation and George asked if it was easy to get work on the railway.

After a few moments silence while they considered this one of the older men replied, a Welsh lilt to his voice. 'Takes a lot of boys to run a railway.' He looked at George shrewdly. 'You after clerical work I should think.'

George was disappointed that he gave that impression but realised that to say he wanted to drive locomotives would sound naïve and probably cause hilarity, so he opted for what was partly the truth. 'I haven't given it much thought 'til today but I'm not really an office type.'

They accepted this without comment and renewed their own conversation, which seemed to concern the domestic life of one of the older men. George walked along with them until, just before the station they turned off down a service road. 'Go over to the office, the GWR one, in the station if you're interested in work. So long.'

George watched them go, the idea of being part of this world away from the closed family business he knew getting stronger, at the same time knowing that reality in the shape of the family and his loyalty to it would probably clip the wings of this flight of fancy. Nevertheless, the sound of a steam whistle drew him into the station as surely as a siren song. He gazed at the huge spans that made the roof, which was the biggest structure he had ever seen. The multiple sounds of station activity echoed around the vast space. George was entranced. He was used to the hectic bustle of Covent Garden but here there was magic in the sight of the steel rails running out into the open, an unbroken link to distant places. A locomotive was standing at the far end of the first platform with its train of carriages strung out behind. George found that by buying a ticket he could get onto the platform. He drifted along the length of the train observing the carriages closely but keeping clear of boarding passengers, until he reached the engine. The machine hissed gently, giving hints of great power held in abeyance. The smells were as new to George as the sights and sounds. A mixture of steam-laden coal smoke, of course, but there were other elements he couldn't easily place. They formed a compound smell that people were getting used to in all large stations. A blend of goods, passengers, gas lighting overlaid by grease and oil. He stood for a while absorbing all this, experiencing a longing to be involved.

The train, he discovered, wasn't due to leave yet so he made his way reluctantly to the office he'd been told about. He stood outside the etched glass panelled door, wondering whether to enter. After a mental struggle he decided not to risk taking precipitate action before at least broaching the subject with the family and this gave him a feeling of relief. After all, he had never needed to apply for a job in his life so had to prepare. At least that's what he told himself.

As he turned to go, the office door opened and a smartly dressed man came onto the platform, his height emphasised by a top hat. He examined a pocket watch and looked up the station to the huge, rounded end framing the daylight beyond. George wondered if this could be the station master, a term he had heard of. He certainly carried an air of authority as he spun round to stride off towards the station concourse.

George waited until the train he'd seen pulled out with all the drama of green flags and whistles and an explosion of noise from the engine. He watched the last carriage disappear and imagined the train rattling and roaring through miles of countryside though to where? He had no idea.

He began the trek back to Primrose Hill, where he intended to examine more closely the premises he'd seen earlier and perhaps make some inquiries regarding the surroundings. He needed something promising to present to his family if he was thinking of deserting.

CHAPTER THIRTEEN

George returned to the family home in Clerkenwell after another look at the Primrose Hill district. He was feeling pleased with himself and optimistic, though still full of ideas concerning his future as a railway worker. He would, he thought, introduce the idea very gently so that when the time came to actually apply for a job the family would have come to accept the plan.

The first obstacle to his project presented itself as he entered the house tired but happy. Vincent, next in age to George, was in the hallway, his right arm in a sling.

'What have you been up to then? Or are you just giving your arm a rest?'

Vincent looked shamefaced as he explained. 'Fell off a cart and broke my collarbone.'

George was concerned but also surprised. Vincent was a fit, agile lad not prone to mishaps.

'I don't know. I'm away for a couple of days and look what happens. How did it happen anyway? You're usually as quick as a monkey.'

'Yeah, too quick. I was helping the Pritchards unload cabbages and caught my foot in a strap they had across the cart. Had to go to St Georges and now I've got to have this sling for weeks. I'm really fed up.'

With the workforce reduced and the possibility of setting up a shop, George realised that his own plans were going to be delayed indefinitely. Though disappointed, he did his best to cheer Vince up by describing his long walk and its hopeful results. He knew how frustrating it was going to be for his energetic brother.

'You're young. It'll mend quickly. We'll get some comfrey tea. That'll do the trick.'

It wasn't until the following day that George could brief his parents, but as soon as he had done so, events moved alarmingly quickly. George soon realised that the project had gripped the family just by virtue of his mission, which they had clearly assumed would be successful. The following morning the routine tidying was hurried through and George and his parents set off for Primrose Hill in the family brougham. The three shared the excitement as they arrived at the place George had discovered and, after inspecting the new buildings and strolling round the few streets in the area, they agreed that the situation looked promising and worth a visit to the appointed solicitors.

A short ride brought them to the law firm of Crabtree and Jordan, where the door was opened by a young clerk who responded with some enthusiasm when he heard the reasons for their visit. In this he was displaying a naivety that Victor shrewdly picked up on. Perhaps there was no great demand for the properties they were interested in. He tucked the thought away as a future bargaining possibility.

The clerk showed them into a very small waiting room and disappeared. Although the room was cramped, with just space for four upright chairs and a low table, there was a tiny fireplace which would give some comfort during the winter but which now displayed a bunch of grasses and daisies. The room that morning was stuffy and there was a faint aroma of cigar smoke in the warm air. Victor opened a sash window although the air outside was as still as that within. The clerk soon returned with the welcome news that Mr Jordan was available to meet them. He led them to another ground floor room and having ostentatiously knocked, ushered them in.

Mr Jordan rose from his seat behind a highly polished and empty desk. Taking a small cloth from a waistcoat pocket he gently wiped a pair of spectacles then, having perched these on his nose, he beamed across the room, carefully taking in all three of his visitors and nodding at each in turn. Drawing on his many years of business, Victor guessed on first sight that the solicitor was no fool. The guests were invited to draw in chairs and seated themselves in a semi-circle facing Mr Jordan's desk whereupon, without a word, he raised his eyebrows and looked enquiringly at Victor.

He listened attentively to Victor's presentation of the family's wholesale trade and their proposed plans. He expressed no sign of approval or the reverse when Victor, with supplementary contributions from Queenie and George, had finished speaking.

He took off his spectacles and began polishing them again, an activity that Queenie had already surmised gave him thinking time to consider a response when required.

'Well,' he began thoughtfully, 'this is a very interesting plan commercially and your interest in the Primrose Hill properties betokens shrewd choice. However, I would think that you will need to be reliant for some time on the original business. For this reason. That the district you have considered will not, I believe, mature for some years.'

Victor leaned forward as if to speak, but Mr Jordan held up a hand.

'But,' and he unexpectedly thumped the desk with a palm, 'I have the idea that there is eventual great promise there for retail enterprises.'

He leaned back in his chair and scrutinised the family group expectantly.

'Well, that's good to hear,' said Victor. He turned to give his wife a glance with the very slightest of winks. 'Of course we will be looking at other possibilities and other districts. We have to get this right what with the capital involved.'

Mr Jordan nodded. He could see that some bargaining lay ahead. He cleared his throat and went to a shelf with files and bundles of papers stacked along its length. He drew out a thin sheaf and brought it over to his desk.

'These are the ground plans of the terrace properties,' he announced, unfolding several sheets.

The family gathered around the desk to examine the documents. George remembered the house at which he had enquired during his tour and could identify it from the drawings. From their earlier visit they could all pinpoint the building that held most potential for their shop and this they pointed out to Mr Jordan. Three of the properties had large crosses pencilled; these were under offer they were told. Theirs was not marked but the adjacent one was, and this was noted by Victor.

'You see, we really could do with two of these buildings and I suppose next door would be most convenient.'

For the first time Mr Jordan showed some surprise. He raised his eyebrows a fraction. He wasn't alone. George and Queenie were taken aback as they realised that Victor had an agenda of his own, which unusually he hadn't shared. There was a halt to the discussion as Mr Jordan considered.

'The adjacent property is under offer but I could approach the buyers to see how fixed they are,' he said finally. He certainly didn't want to lose the chance of selling two items while Victor was pursuing his other possibilities. He couldn't remember if his other clients had a particular reason for their choice but he could find out. He assumed the price was not a factor, since all the properties in the terrace were marked at between £850 and £900. George was still absorbing this. The higher finances of the family had, he saw, been kept between Victor and Queenie.

The negotiations ended with Victor offering £1500 for separated properties or £200 more for the two that were adjacent. Mr Jordan promised to let them know as soon as he could whether both options were possible and if the vendors, who were the original developers, would be in a position to accept either offer.

Victor, Queenie and George drove home in silence, each with their own thoughts and feelings mixed between excitement and apprehension regarding what they were about to undertake.

CHAPTER FOURTEEN
– Gloucester 2017

———•———

'Are you seeing Miss Copeland, sir?'

Peter paused his packing away. 'Seeing?'

The two sixth form boys he knew well from the Science Group looked at each other.

'OK, let's say I am. Boy, news still gets around quickly by word of mouth, or is it quicker by Facebook?'

'We just wanted to say we were pleased, sir, and we hope it works out. Miss Copeland's a good teacher and popular.'

Their good wishes were touching, though he tried not to let that show.

'What's her trick then?' he asked. 'I could do with some tips.'

'She's funny. She makes us all laugh,' said Simon.

Peter was intrigued, and although he knew he really shouldn't ask, the temptation was too great.

'How on earth does she do that then?'

'She does mimes. Like invents scenarios for them. And it's not like "look how clever I am" it's so natural. Good teaching too. You look forward to her little plays so language lessons aren't dull and it's amazing how much you can remember from them.'

Peter, in fact, remembered the 'little play' with the umbrella.

'Yes, I've seen a bit of that. Well thanks for your well-wishing. Watch this space, as they say.'

Peter was not meeting Julie that evening, and on the way home he ran over what the two lads had told him. Her classroom technique fascinated him. How amazing that anyone could do those things. He would never have the courage, and even if he tried it would be an embarrassing fiasco.

Julie had also caught wind of student awareness of their getting together but thought she'd wait for Peter to make his own discovery rather than mention it. She remembered with amusement the keen interest that some of her contemporaries had taken in staff affairs when she'd been at school, so she should have expected to be an object of interest.

During the last two weeks of the spring term they met sporadically, though most of the weekend was spent together. Amongst other things, they went over activities relating to the Science Group. From time to time Julie brooded in a vague way about her dream experiences and wished she could connect them to a real event in some way in the manner Paul had. She carried out disjointed searches on the internet but realised that there was not much to go on. Someone had lost something and water was involved and that was it. She read about various sea disasters, the list of which seemed endless. If the oceans were suddenly drained, she thought, there would be thousands of ship remains to explore. Anyway, the vista that appeared in her dream wasn't a seascape, unless perhaps it showed a harbour or, say, a sea loch or fjord. She talked to Peter about it occasionally but really had nothing new to say and she could see there was a danger of becoming a bore on this topic. He hinted as much a couple of times but in truth he was concerned that she was thinking about it too much. He was starting to wish Paul had never triggered the thing in the first place.

As it happened the dream experience was far from Julie's thoughts when she did strike gold. She'd been reading an article on climate change in a magazine. In the same edition there were a few related articles and she'd been gazing at the reproduction of a sketch showing a fair held on the river Thames during something called a mini-ice age. The text explained that this had occurred before the river was hemmed in by wharves and embankments so that the ice formed much more easily in the shallow water. She flipped through a few more pages, glimpsing as she did so a print of another painting. She turned back to look at it. The shock she felt luckily wasn't sudden. It crept over her in stages. First came a strong emotion of recognition and familiarity. Then disbelief, and last a desire to know what this image was about. She looked down at the caption. She read that on the 15 January 1867, there had been a disaster at the lake in Regent's Park, London. Forty skaters had died when the ice gave way beneath them.

She sat gazing at the image for some minutes. It was, she reasoned, only an artist's impression, but the likeness to her recollected dream image was strong. She began an analysis of the picture to try to see what features had made such an impression. There were buildings in the background and she assumed that the artist had been faithful to the skyline. In the foreground the shape of the lake's shore looked familiar. It wasn't much she realised, but then why had a first glance attracted her attention? There was the essential element of water and of course enormous loss for many people.

Julie felt strangely unreal. Nerve endings tingled up and down her back as she tried to absorb the radical possibility that echoes of an event could somehow float around to be picked up by someone remote in space and time. She knew what most scientists would say to that. And if such things were possible then whose memories had caused that faint resonance in her infant brain? Those resonances had given her a picture that was static. A view possibly of a lake from a vantage point near its shore. But the lake was empty and the view was accompanied by an emotion. A loss; a longing. What if, she thought, a survivor had returned to the scene, perhaps to mourn? Julie put down the magazine and went to her window. She contrasted her peaceful sunlit street to the horror of that far off winter day. She could imagine the screams and shouts of the skaters and the helplessness of the watchers. Was she in any way linked to this? She was going to have to find everything there was to know about this disaster.

CHAPTER FIFTEEN

---•---

'When did you say this happened?'

Julie was relating to Peter what little she had found out about the lake tragedy.

'1867.'

'Phew, that would be a long time for a trace memory; if such things exist.'

'Of course.' Julie felt slightly irritated. 'I hope you're not going to start getting sceptical just when it's getting interesting. Anyway, if such a thing can happen, who says it weakens with time?'

Peter immediately regretted the impression he had given, but now he too was faced with something that he considered pretty farfetched and he was not going to go along with it without reservations, even at the risk of annoying Julie. There was a silence while they both contemplated a disagreement.

So far they had enjoyed the Easter break. They had agreed to spend a few days walking on the Cotswold Way. Julie hadn't mentioned the lake disaster for the first few days to allow time for her own ideas to settle. Even though she was expecting some resistance from Peter, now it had happened she was disappointed. She broke the ensuing silence.

'OK so you find the whole thing improbable, perhaps a fantasy, and I have the same doubts. But I have to balance those against what I felt and still feel. I can't ignore it.'

They were sitting on the bench in Julie's garden after a day walking and a bus ride home from Cheltenham. Peter leaned back and looked at the mass of new cherry blossom, which he thought almost obscenely beautiful.

'I'm really sorry. Can we start again with this one? Tell me how much you've been able to find out.'

'You're sure you want to hear? This may be a journey I have to make alone, me being the only player.'

'Yes. I definitely want to hear. And if you're the only player I'm sure I can be a useful supporter.'

Mollified, Julie began to relate what the internet had given her. A description of the accident, a list of those drowned and the work of recovering the bodies, which proved difficult. Peter was shocked by the scale and nature of the disaster and was amazed that it could happen within a large city. Was there no guidance given on safety?

'That's one of the interesting things,' said Julie. 'A day before, there was a small incident involving the ice breaking, but there were no casualties and notices had been put up giving warnings. And they were just ignored and either there were no officials around that afternoon or they thought the ice was solid enough. Huge changes were made afterwards. The whole lake was drained and the depth, which had been twelve feet, that's about three and a half metres, was reduced to one and a half metres.'

'That must have been quite a job,' said Peter.

'Well, they didn't want to take any chances and anyway, no one was allowed on the lake ever again.'

'So what's your next move? I really would like to help.'

Julie smiled. 'Just support without too many objections will be great. First I want a trip to London and a visit to Regents Park. How about it?'

'We've got next week off. We could make a day of it; maybe find a concert or show.'

'I'll try to find something. Meantime perhaps I need to do some research into my family tree. See who was around in Victorian times and find out where they were.'

'I see what you're getting at. Just as Paul had a possible familial link with his dream.'

'Yes. Though Paul had no further experiences after visiting his disaster site. Still, no stone unturned, and wouldn't it be exciting if there was some kind of connection? I bet you'd be a bit less sceptical then.'

'That's a sure bet.' Peter leaned over and gave Julie what he hoped was a reconciliatory kiss and went off to make a delayed pot of tea. In spite of his initial doubts he now felt a stirring of curiosity, but he would certainly try to maintain normal scientific objectivity. That would surely be in Julie's interest.

CHAPTER SIXTEEN
– London 1860

———•———

Early in November a letter arrived for Victor from the solicitor. Delivered by hand, it let him know that their bid had been successful, though they would have to settle for the non-adjacent buildings. This was thrilling news for the family and planning for the move began immediately. Payment for the two properties was to be in four instalments, which Victor initiated during a visit to his bank, after which keys were collected. A day was cleared for a visit and the Yeoman family entered their future premises for the first time. The weather was not encouraging. Although midway through November a warm muggy drizzle blanketed the district so the dry solidity of the new buildings was welcome. The rooms echoed their footsteps and voices as they explored and gazed around. The smell of newness in timbers and paintwork addressed them, inviting them to share a beginning. 'Well here we are; what are you going to make of us?'

'I hope we're doing the right thing,' murmured Queenie.

'Hey up, girl, we can't go wrong,' returned Victor though he too was wondering whether he had been completely mad to ever start on this course. After all, they could have plodded on with their familiar lives at the garden indefinitely. But no; this was a venture and an adventure. If it went wrong it wouldn't be the end for them, since their old business would be intact, hopefully.

Winter passed with the usual delays and hardship during snowfalls. George and Annie, his sister, were assigned to run the new shop and visits were frequent as they got on with the fitting out. Annie would be living above the shop and George would occupy the other premises, three doors away. Victor cautiously leaked information to others in both wholesale and retail trade. Reactions were mixed and of course there were elements of suspicion, but to the family's relief acceptance ruled and there was no marked hostility. Curiosity there was, however. Although there were many overt good wishes for success, Victor suspected that there would not be too much sympathy if his experiment failed. People were like that, he reckoned, even good friends.

Towards the end of winter there came a suggestion from the Hopkin's farm that perhaps they could deliver part of their regular supplies directly to the new shop. Since the distance was not great they could bring produce more frequently, possibly extending the range they could offer. Victor suggested that George pay the farm a visit to discuss arrangements. George hadn't mentioned to his family his previous trip, the aim of which had been to enquire after Tillie Hopkins, and he felt slightly embarrassed. He wasn't to know that his father and Adrian Hopkins had already derived some mild if sympathetic amusement about his romantic venture during one of the farm's deliveries. To balance that, however, George had not mentioned his active interest in railways with the possibility of a career change. It occurred to him that by taking on the business trip to the farm he might make contact with Tillie's fiancée, which could be of benefit in the future. This thought he kept to himself.

The opening day for the shop was approaching when George set out on foot for the Hopkin's farm. He was alone but, as it turned out, accompanied by good fortune regarding his secret mission. A mile from the farm he spotted a short but powerfully built man in overalls. The man was just about to leap over a stile but George, chancing his luck, called out sharply enough to interrupt the jump. Surely given his looks and apparel, and that he had just walked from the direction of the farm, he was the man he wanted to meet, and even if he wasn't no harm would be done. The man waited and George increased his pace to avoid delay. It was clearly up to George to open the conversation.

'My name's George Yeoman and I have business with Mr and Mrs Hopkins this morning,' he began somewhat formally. 'I hoped you might be acquainted with them.'

The man smiled and nodded slowly as he looked George over.

'Well, well.' He paused. 'George Yeoman.' His smile broadened. 'I'm hoping you haven't come to steal away my intended.' His rolling Welsh accent was full of humour and his smile broke into a chuckle as he saw George's startled expression.

'Oh. So you've heard about my last visit here. I'm mortified. I'd no idea she was spoken for.'

65

'No need at all. It just shows we both have good taste in young ladies.'

Reassured, George held out his hand, which the other grasped firmly.

'Dafydd Morgan, pleased to meet you.'

George noted the hardness of the man's hands, the result of several years stoking the fireboxes of locomotives no doubt. The thought prompted him to take advantage of this opportunity.

'Actually, I've been hoping to meet you to talk about railways.'

'Railways. Well there's a big subject, but you'll have to walk a way with me since the railway's where I'm off to now.'

They crossed the stile and began walking the footpath that traversed the field and several more in the London direction.

'So what is it about railways then?' Dafydd stopped and seized George's arm and laughed. 'I know. You want to be an engine driver!'

'Silly I suppose. It suddenly came upon me as I did my tour looking for shop premises how amazing it was. Not just the locomotives but the way the railway lines are spreading out and linking far off places. The stations, noise, smells. But yes, it must be wonderful to be in charge of those great machines.'

George was thankful to find that Dafydd wasn't going to make fun of him. Rather he looked thoughtful.

'It is wonderful. Nothing like it. But it's not easy to get there. I had a couple of hard years, hard and grimy years, before I started as fireman. That's where I'm at still and two more years before I can hope to go up to driver. But you get to know the whole job first. Cleaning, oiling, raking out and getting up early to wake the crews. That or starting the fire and building up steam pressure. Better than the coal mines I escaped from though. But look, we don't have the time now. How would you feel about helping me with roofing a barn at the farm? If we can get time off we can talk railways and your prospects while we work. I tried to get some done this morning but it's slow on my own.'

George was pleased with this invitation and provisional arrangements were made. He walked back across the field and on to the farm, all the time remembering Dafydd's words 'your prospects'. He hoped at first that his new acquaintance wouldn't mention his interest in railways to anyone, but on reflection perhaps some hint or other might make things easier with family later on. Dafydd, meanwhile, on his resumed walk to work, had no intention of discussing George's ideas with anyone. His own break with family in the South Wales valleys had taught him the value of discretion.

CHAPTER SEVENTEEN

———◆———

Dafydd was high on the barn roof by the time George arrived at the farm, having earlier let Annie know where he was spending the day. He was hoping this new freedom would continue when the shop opened, as his sister and he could take turns at serving and otherwise running the business.

'Bore da, that's good morning to you. How are you on heights? Don't worry if you're not happy up here. You'll still be useful.'

'Reckon I'll be all right.'

George tested the single ladder for stability and climbed competently but steadily. Dafydd watched approvingly. From their first meeting and continuing now, George had the feeling that Dafydd was going to be in a friendly older brother role. It would need getting used to if this was to be the case. George was the older brother in his family. When they were both perched on the exposed beams and planks, Dafydd explained the repairs he was making to the roof timbers and pointed out the tiles that he'd taken off and would be replacing.

'Extremely heavy. That's why the roof has to be good,' said Dafydd.

They began working with George fetching and carrying and holding timber firmly for Dafydd to saw and drill. Mrs Hopkins came over with Tillie as the morning wore on, bringing two bowls of stew and thick slices of bread. If Tillie was aware of George's one-time quest she gave no sign of it and greeted him in a gay, friendly manner. They resumed work, chatting when they could. George was curious about how Dafydd had met Tillie, but was only promised an account later.

'Tell me about Covent Garden.'

George was wondering when they could talk about railways and was impatient to ask about his 'prospects', but had to be content with relating the workings of the great wholesale market. It may have been tedious to him but Dafydd seemed interested in the smallest details. George was to discover this to be a main feature of the Welshman's character. Early in the afternoon jugs of fruit-flavoured water were brought out with a plate of oat biscuits.

'No alcohol while you're up there mind,' said Mrs Hopkins.

'No indeed, nor tonight when I'm on the footplate,' replied Dafydd.

'You mean you'll work here all day then work a train?' exclaimed George.

'It's just a local and we'll be packing up here soon. In fact,' said Dafydd looking around, 'let's knock off now. We'll go down and have a proper talk.'

They made safe the tools and climbed down to sit on rough crates amid the miscellaneous farm items stored in the barn. Pleasant though unidentifiable farm odours drifted around them.

'How I met Tillie is linked to railways. That's why I didn't start on it before. You'd only have started pestering me about your hopes. Am I right?'

George nodded wryly.

'Well all in good time. It happened like this. She'd been off to visit relatives near Staines. Returning on a train I was working. No inkling of that mind. Until she walked past the engine carrying two heavy bags from her aunt. Some sort of weaving apparatus. Luckily, the train had been packed and no porters were free just then. She put the stuff down right opposite me, clearly needing a rest. I was just about to go off and so quickly checking with my driver, I hopped down and walked over to her. I really don't know what came over me but turning on my full Welsh charm, which of course is considerable, I asked if I could assist. Immediately bowled over of course, she gratefully accepted. By the time we reached the road I was deeply in love and there you have it. Love gave me courage and I asked if I could visit her. Why she should have come round to love a poor greasy fireman is a mystery but I'm not going to argue with destiny.'

George was delighted with the story and almost forgot his own concerns in picturing the platform meeting. 'That's a great story. It was obviously meant to be. I'll keep a look out when I'm on the footplate.'

'So you are still thinking of that. Well, as I said, it's a hard slog and you start at the bottom with bottom wages as well. But see here, why don't you consider other options? You'd still be close to the trains. You can read and write, also arithmetic from your family business. There's good clerical jobs; clean and better paid.'

George was disappointed. He didn't know what he'd been expecting from Dafydd or what would be realistic. Perhaps this was good advice. After all, to be involved in the huge railway adventure must be exciting. He thought about the trains that were at this moment steaming through the countryside. You didn't have to be driving them to feel a part of it; the small drama as a train left the station or the excitement on an empty platform when one was due.

'Whatever you try I'll help if I can,' said Dafydd, not wanting George to be too despondent. 'But I suppose you'd better get this shop going first. I'm hoping to meet the rest of your family at the wedding.'

George was startled and Dafydd, pleased to have surprised him, chuckled.

'You'll be getting your invitation soon,' he said.

CHAPTER EIGHTEEN

———◆———

A May wedding was planned and the Yeomans were pleased to be invited, along with various members of the farming community. Dafydd had, with some misgivings, let his family in the Welsh valleys know about it but was doubtful that they would make the journey. He hadn't left Wales on the best of terms and had sometimes felt like a deserter which, he supposed, he was. In the meantime the Yeoman grocery shop opened with a minimum of ceremony. It was clear from the outset that the choice of location had been at least prudent and at best wildly successful. The expanding residential population of the area included many homes provided for railway workers and ascended to large residences for a middle-class community. A leaflet was dropped in a few hundred letterboxes with word of mouth left to do the rest. Annie and George had decided to offer a wide range of produce but were careful not to overstock. No one could be more aware of the perishable nature of their goods. They aimed to be open from half-past eight in the morning until six o'clock. Their first customer was waiting on the doorstep on the first morning; a housemaid sent out by her mistress to assess the new shop as well as to purchase vegetables. She also had orders to inquire about the possibility of opening an account.

'Oh, and my mistress would like to know about deliveries; not today of course.'

During preparations for the shop these matters had been discussed so George and Annie were well prepared. Unknown of course were the numbers expected, so they might well be overwhelmed by delivery requirements. In which case they would either have to call a younger member of the family away from the city or hire a part-time delivery boy. With regard to customer accounts they would not refuse anyone but, since their knowledge of the area had yet to be acquired, they determined to be strict in the manner of end-of-month payments.

Ella, as the housemaid introduced herself, chose her vegetables and unfolded a strong bag, into which they were tumbled straight from the brand-new scales. She paid with coins from an apron pocket and walked to the open door, turning before leaving with a smile.

'I'm glad you're here,' she said and disappeared.

Perhaps she detected the anxiety felt by Annie and George. He had been fussing about the shelves while Annie served and with the shop empty for a few moments the two new staff turned to each other with expressions of relief. The shop was underway and though they were unused to dealing directly with the public they were suddenly confident.

This was to be their new life, and although strange at first they both soon settled into a routine. They were now much closer to the public and their lives than they had been in Covent Garden. As day by day new customers arrived they found that their horizons grew. Some customers were frequent and these they were getting to know well. Many of the buyers were from the domestic staff of well-off families, but these were outnumbered by the wives of ordinary working men. There was a universal view that more shops were needed in the area. It occurred to George and Annie that other retail traders might take an interest following their example. Many were the complaints that there were long treks for meat and dairy produce. It transpired that there were deliveries to be carried out almost every day so the resulting division of labour meant that Annie spent most time in the shop while George was out delivering. At first these journeys were more time consuming than he would have liked but familiarity with the district and consequent better planning sped them up.

The arrangement with the Hopkins farm, though not part of the original plan, proved a great help. Their deliveries to the shop reduced the work of bringing stock from the city. It also gave George a chance to meet up with Dafydd when he had a lift with the farm cart on his way to work. They had finished the repairs to the barn together before the opening of the shop and since they got on well together, George intended to show Dafydd around the London he knew but that his friend might not. He assumed, though, that free time for Dafydd once he was married might be harder to find.

CHAPTER NINETEEN

———•———

Hot dry weather set in during the week before Tillie and Dafydd's wedding and George for the first time in the year was longing to get up to the Hampstead ponds, but on the Tuesday he had arranged the afternoon off to meet Dafydd at Paddington Station at the time when, with luck, his train would be arriving. Wear some overalls, Dafydd had said, to avoid looking like a passenger. He wouldn't say more and George was looking forward to being close to a locomotive again. By the time he arrived, with the unaccustomed weight of overalls from the shop's store, he was hot enough to be thinking of the ponds again and hoping that Dafydd would be free to join him for a swim.

Armed with a platform ticket he gratefully rested on a seat with a Great Western plaque and awaited the train, which eventually pulled in eighteen minutes late. There was a flurry of passengers and porters for a few minutes, following which the platform was empty and the coaches stood deserted with their doors swung open. Dafydd waved and beckoned George over. The driver climbed down, tipped his cap to George and strolled towards the station concourse.

'Quick now, pull yourself up,' instructed Dafydd above the hissing noises from the engine.

George was delighted and grabbed the handrail to climb onto the footplate.

'Just a couple of minutes or I might get into trouble,' said Dafydd with a grin.

Instantly another world. A steel cell raised high above the platform with a wall full of levers, dials and gauges, the space permeated by coal dust and steam. Dafydd opened the shutter to show George the furnace still glowing fiercely. He pointed to a large round dial mounted just above head height on the front wall of the cab.

'That's the vital thing now. Steam pressure. If that drops too much the train won't climb the uphill gradients.'

George peered from one of the small side windows.

'How do you see ahead clearly?'

Dafydd shrugged. 'It's not always easy and you have to concentrate hard at times, but you get used to it.'

'Is there a lot of movement like rocking. How smooth is it?'

'That's interesting because you see, this is a wide-gauge engine. A lot of the railways setting up are using track where the rails are closer together. I haven't been on one of those but I've heard that everything on those tracks is a lot less stable at speed. There's a battle going on between the two systems. We can only have one of them if the country is to standardise. I hope they go for this one.'

At that point the driver returned. He waited while George climbed back to the normal world after a last longing gaze round the cab.

Dafydd called down from the footplate. 'Hope you've time to wait. I'll be about an hour. We have to get this old girl to the shed.'

George nodded. Another engine had been coupled to the coaches ready to haul them out of the station and a guard was walking along the platform slamming the doors shut.

George wandered round the station, enjoying the sounds and smells until Dafydd turned up.

'Fancy a swim?'

For the first time since he'd known him, Dafydd seemed taken aback.

'I never learned to swim, George.'

This was unexpected.

'I can maybe help you to pick it up. Anyway you don't have to get out of your depth at the ponds and it would be refreshing in this weather.'

With some reservation Dafydd agreed and they set out to trudge to Hampstead. George guided them to a secluded spot and began undressing.

'What am I to wear?' Dafydd asked.

'Nothing. Look there's no one around.'

George waded into the shallows and gratefully sank to his neck. Dafydd was not going to be outdone and followed. He had to admit that it felt wonderfully cool after sweating in the engine for half the day.

'Tillie's going to be very annoyed if you get me drowned, you know.'

George ignored him.

'Look, get down to your shoulders and sweep your arms forward and round.' George demonstrated. 'Can you feel you can move forward like that? Just keep doing that for a bit then try to lift maybe one leg off the mud.'

After ten minutes and some noisy spluttering Dafydd seemed to be making progress and said he was feeling more confident. George was satisfied and swam out into the lake, though he kept a watch on his pupil. Dafydd soon tired and climbed out. He laid out his clothes on the dry parched ground and lay down totally relaxed. George swam up and down the lake a few times then joined him. They lay in the comforting shade, refreshed and at peace, thankfully remote from the busy world for a short time.

CHAPTER TWENTY

———✦———

They were strolling towards their respective homes when Dafydd pointed to a hand-printed sign pinned to a fence.

'Can you read that from here, George?'

George squinted for a few seconds but could only hazard guesses, some of which were incorrect.

'Remember this afternoon when you were looking through the porthole and asked whether it was easy to see the line ahead and any obstructions or signals? The thing is, I'm not sure your eyesight would be sharp enough to drive or fire a locomotive. They do test for distance vision. As a fireman I have lookout responsibilities as well as the driver. Sorry to say this, and I could be wrong, but it's best to be warned.'

George considered this. He felt disappointed but it hadn't come as a complete shock. Over the years he had suspected that both his parents possessed better distance vision than his.

'Don't worry about it. Anyway I've been thinking on the advice you gave me. There are probably lots of jobs on the railways that I could be happy with. There's something about stations I like, with always something going on. Changing the subject, is everything ready for the wedding?'

'Pretty much, I hope. It's only a small affair. Farmwork doesn't allow much of a break. We've decided to go down to Wales just after. Hope to patch up a bit with my family with Tillie as a help.'

'You haven't told me where you'll both be living,' said George.

'No, well we'll be looking for somewhere to rent but there's room at the farm 'til then.'

After parting with Dafydd George walked on thoughtfully. He was thinking of the house he was occupying at the moment. He wasn't sure why his parents had bought the second property and he wasn't sure they knew. One idea was that the ground floor would be storage, but another that it would accommodate more of the family. At the moment there was no real reason why he should live there except maybe to keep it warm and aired. It could be bringing in some rent and provide a first home for Dafydd and Tillie. He would broach the matter with his parents. After the wedding they might be more likely to consider the idea favourably.

The wedding was a modest but joyful event. George and his parents and siblings, apart from Annie, who had to remain at the shop, arrived at the church in good time. There were guests from the various branches of Tillie's family who mingled with local members of the farming community. Dafydd had hired a smart frock coat with trousers, together with a top hat, and with a borrowed cane to complete the picture he was clearly enjoying the occasion immensely. He had a word for everyone, which included of course Hopkins family members he had never met, who were all taken by his, as he had once described it to George, considerable Welsh charm.

Tillie was all radiance and her wedding dress the object of much admiration. She had long ago let her aunt know of her part in her niece's destiny as it was while returning from a visit that the meeting at Paddington Station had occurred. Since millinery was Aunt Annabel's occupation there was clearly no one else better suited to design and make the wedding dress.

It was inevitable that during the day George would once or twice find himself wishing that he'd met Tillie before Dafydd had and that he might have been standing at the altar instead of his friend. However, the friendship had become far too strong to dwell on such thoughts and he sincerely wished for great happiness for them both. A few weeks before the wedding Dafydd had confided to George that he had not been the only competition for Tillie's attention and that he'd experienced several unpleasant exchanges touching on his Welsh nationality. As an answer to how he'd reacted, Dafydd had merely shown George a clenched fist. It brought home to George how he'd much rather have Dafydd as a friend than an enemy. He was also able to see how the very qualities he so much admired in Dafydd, his strength, experience and maturity, were also those that attracted Tillie.

After the ceremony there was plenty of food and drink laid out in the barn that George and Dafydd had repaired. Several guests expressed disappointment that none of Dafydd's family had come and he explained that he and Tillie would be meeting them in the next day or two. The newly weds departed with Tillie's father driving the carriage. They had booked to stay at a hotel near Paddington Station, from where they would travel by train to the west. Dafydd was looking forward to a comfortable ride with no responsibilities. Back at the farm those guests not staying the night departed well pleased.

Chapter Twenty-one

———•———

By the time the newlyweds were due to return, George had obtained his parents' approval to offer them what was in fact the spare house. He went over to the farm within a week to present his idea.

'Well I can't say it hadn't occurred to me as well,' said Dafydd. 'I couldn't help wondering what it was going to be used for.'

'It certainly hadn't occurred to me, though I do think it's a wonderful idea. When can we move in?' Tillie was delighted.

'Hold your horses, Tillie. We have to give it some thought.'

'Oh, come on husband. Who'd have thought I'd be married to such a stuffed shirt?'

Tillie's eyes twinkled as she put her arm round Dafydd's waist.

'There might be a few things to consider though,' said George. 'We will, for example, need a room on the ground floor for storage sometimes.'

'That's all right. I grew up on the farm so I'm used to sharing my home with a few tons of onions. Anyway, Dafydd and I can always hold our grand balls somewhere else.'

There was clearly no way to curb Tillie's enthusiasm and the arrangements were agreed on the spot.

And thus, within just a year, the lives of two families had changed drastically. The only sadness was that felt by Tillie's parents on the day she trundled away from the farm for the last time with a small cart carrying her few possessions and some domestic items for the new home. New patterns of life were established amongst the demands of work. At first Tillie put aside thoughts of earning money and set about creating a welcoming home for Dafydd and any of the new friends she hoped to make in the area. The houses had yards at the back that contained an outdoor toilet. The idea that you could flush your waste away with hardly a thought fascinated Tillie.

'Where does it all go?' she wanted to know. But the labyrinthine workings of the new sewerage systems seemed known only to those involved in their design and construction, leaving most people grateful but unconcerned.

Tillie was delighted with the yard, which she felt was homely and manageable compared with the wide spaces of the farm. Over the summer she collected stones, seeds and pots to transform the original bare space. During September she realised, after initial doubts, that her first baby would be arriving during the following spring and future activities would need this taken into account. It had become a routine for Dafydd and Tillie to take walks with George and Annie on Sunday afternoons. They would sometimes reflect together, given the turbulent times, how lucky they were to be financially secure, even if not wealthy. That Tillie could look forward to her firstborn without the struggle many women had to endure. Their prayers of thanks during the morning services were heartfelt.

During their visit to Wales Dafydd had related the story of the Yeoman's expansion to his family and that had travelled to the nearby dairy farm run by the Griffith family. The account had inspired the family to think about their own similar situation, with surplus sons reaching maturity. As a result, Dafydd received an unexpected visit in late August from the father and eldest son, who were looking round for somewhere to start a retail dairy in the same way the Yeomans had done with their greengrocery. They had come first to London and Primrose Hill simply because they knew Dafydd. Unlike his own family, they had never censured him for leaving the area, where the pits were the likely destination for most young men.

Following a friendly evening during which, much to Tillie's annoyance, a good deal of the conversation was conducted in Welsh, the Griffiths were shown the area together with George and Annie's shop.

'Of course it would be different to here,' said the senior Griffith. 'We wouldn't be supplying most of the stock from Wales, though I expect Dafydd here would be able to help with the hard cheeses on his trains.'

'There's no doubt the railways are going to change trading drastically. We'll certainly do our best for you,' promised Dafydd.

And so, on a prominent corner, the Griffith Dairy came to be, thus adding a new strand to a developing neighbourhood having its own networks, resources, characters and leaders and laying the roots for a community.

CHAPTER TWENTY-TWO

Yeoman's soon became a familiar part of the Primrose Hill district. As was the plan, the shop was easy to run since there was little to think about regarding stock. The Covent Garden branch of the family delivered every few days a variety of fruit and vegetables from the wholesale stock and the best produce was always selected. This was particularly helpful during the winter as delays in deliveries were common and the family shop would always be given preference if goods were in short supply. Tillie's parents, of course, had an extra incentive for bringing goods to the shop since they could usually meet their daughter.

Tillie herself was feeling relieved that two months or so of morning sickness had abated, but suffered spells of boredom during the winter. She would often spend time at the Yeoman's house, especially when Dafydd was away on the long shifts that his job necessitated. Occasionally, but with increasing frequency, she would give Annie a break and serve in the shop. This, as Annie and George realised, helped her pass the time and was a way for her to meet some of the customers. She would sometimes sit with Annie or George in the back room behind the shop for a warming drink. At such times George, enjoying the warmth of her company, found himself wishing, as he had at the wedding, that he'd visited the Hopkin's farm before her fateful meeting with Dafydd. But then, he reasoned, he would never have met Dafydd, whose friendship and company he valued highly. He mocked himself for these ridiculous musings, which he kept to himself. He was looking forward to seeing the baby, thinking perhaps that, though not related, he could be an uncle figure, since he or she was going to be short of real uncles.

Tillie's parents knew of several women who practiced midwifery and decided to engage the one they thought would suit their daughter. They would not hear of Dafydd paying her fees and when Lilian was born without problems they were pleased to have contributed to the event. The aunt who had made the wedding dress turned her skills to tiny garments. These were elaborate and highly decorated so that very soon Tillie was lamenting how quickly Lilian grew too big for them.

'Don't fret. They'll do for the next one,' said Dafydd confidently.

Secretly, Tillie hoped that wouldn't be too soon. Many were the women chained to an endless cycle of giving birth, which brought poverty to many families, and although Dafydd earned regular wages they were never going to be rich. She was grateful that he rarely drank ale or stronger, though she never knew whether it was his work that called for abstention or a strong Welsh Chapel upbringing. A bit of each was all he would say.

CHAPTER TWENTY-THREE
– Extracts from Jean Harris' diary, London 1860

October 23

What a joy. To hear Mr Charles Dickens read from a book I have read, or mostly read. I went last night to the music hall in Camden Town with fear I wouldn't be let in – a poor housemaid. But my shilling's as good as anyone's though harder won and scraped together. During the time when Luke was teaching him and me to read I collected from all over magazines to practice. After I found a bit of Oliver Twist I had to find more and though I found other bits by Mr Dickens I had real feelings for that one, and that was what he read from. What a great man with his close observation of life. And such beautiful use of words. I am resolve now to keep a diary to practise how to write. It is such freedom as there's no one I can tell my true feelings, especially my employers. I would be dismissed. No one else close to me either. But to be able to write it down. My heart is full of thanks to my brother for giving me liberty.

November 11

For the first time since starting work for Mr and Mrs Duffield I am unsettled. Housemaid work was new to me when I arrived in London and it took time to get used to how hard it was. Six in the morning until nine at night. But there were books in the library I was allowed to read and with this help and the small dictionary that Luke gave me before I left I am learning so much about my own language. But Mr Duffield's mother has now come, which has been talked about for a long time. At once I can see difficulties for me. There is extra work in keeping her comfortable and when she does get around the house she is already scolding me for something. I am in tears a lot and cannot complain so I am going to look somewhere else.

November 19

I am in my new place, which I saw advertised just last week. I lost money by leaving immediately but the old lady seemed to hate me, so I just wanted to escape. I am working for a widow with a son and daughter living at home. Mrs Denbridge. She seems stern but at least I know what to do and the two children don't interfere. This house was once in the countryside but is being drawn into town by all the development here. It is next to Primrose Hill, which is a nice place to walk when I have time.

December 15

This is such a cold house now winter has set in. My feet itch and the only time I can be warm is when I light or tend the fires in Mrs Denbridge's bedroom and the drawing room. Perhaps it is the cold but her behaviour to me is often quite nasty if I do something not to her liking, which wasn't the case at first. I have spoken to other housemaids when I go out on an errand and only one of them is happy in the employment. Most of them don't stay long in a job so there are always advertisements put up by people wanting maids. It is the frustration that bites into me. Even though I'm young I have known more hardship and poverty than these people will ever know. But I can't tell them or answer back.

December 28

Christmas was miserable and hard work for me. There were visitors from the family and though she wasn't rude to me in front of them she was aloof and demanding. I did get one day off and met up with another servant. We walked over Regents Park to see the ducks on the lake. They were happier than us. I will try to find another post soon. It would be lovely to work for kind employers.

CHAPTER TWENTY-FOUR

S ince the birth of Lilian, Tillie helped in the shop less and at the same time the business became busier. George and Annie were required to work full time to keep it going. There were times when they were both needed to serve but, and they soon knew roughly when they would occur, there were long slack times when either of them could carry out the deliveries and other routine work.

Many of the customers were housemaids from nearby homes and it was during a quiet time one afternoon that one of the regular maids entered the shop clearly in a distressed state. George knew her as Jean and that she had been a customer for over a year. George retreated to the back room, feeling grateful that Annie was on duty. Faced with an upset woman he doubted he had the sensitivity to be a good comforter. Perhaps with a man he might be better.

Annie at once asked what her trouble was, which brought on an increase in Jean's weeping. After hesitating for a moment, George went back into the shop and indicated that Annie should take Jean to the back. Annie shot a grateful glance and guided Jean into the back room. In the absence of further customers George fussed around the displays and eventually began sweeping the floor, though this was hardly needed. He couldn't avoid hearing snatches of the conversation between Annie and Jean, so gathered that it was the treatment handed out by her employer that was the main problem. After a few minutes both women re-entered the shop area and Annie hastily supplied the maid with her requirements. Jean rushed from the shop, alarming Tillie, who had just arrived at the door with Lilian in tow.

'She's upset,' Annie stated as Tillie looked questioningly from the departing woman to Annie. 'To do with her work.'

'Some of the people round here, and probably everywhere else, take advantage of their servants,' said Tillie, guessing at the problem.

Annie felt that she ought to treat the details of what Jean had told her as confidential so kept Jean's tale back from Tillie.

Jean had woken up that morning feeling quite ill and had got behind with her schedule of work in spite of beginning shortly after five o'clock. The woman who employed her had been angry enough not only to launch a tirade of shouting but had actually gripped Jean's arms and shaken her. Jean was shocked and carried on with her work automatically, though dazed. It was only when she reached the shop and encountered Annie and George that her emotions caught up with her.

Annie and Tillie went on discussing the servant issue for a few minutes. George was keeping an eye on Lilian, who had staggered over to a box of carrots and had begun an inspection, picking up and replacing carrots one at a time. He was listening to the conversation and wondering if they could help the unfortunate housemaid. The Yeomans had always employed one or two domestic staff at the family home, which was useful as so much of their working lives involved physical labour and long days. But at the moment no one was employed at either of the Primrose Hill premises. For some time he'd been brooding on that issue and, it must be said, linking it in some way to his own ambitions.

When Tillie had left he suggested to Annie that they have a discussion after the shop closed. Annie was puzzled but George couldn't be drawn to explain and soon left to deliver a sack of turnips and potatoes. On his return he lit the fire in the range. Not for the first time he thought about the time he and his sister spent on domestic tasks. After locking up George explained, with no preamble, his desire to leave the family business. Annie experienced a mixture of shock and curiosity.

'Railways,' she exclaimed. 'How did you get to that?'

George explained how he'd become interested as he travelled around looking for a site for the shop, which included his visit to Paddington and the developing friendship with Dafydd that had nurtured the fascination. He described with enthusiasm standing on the footplate of Dafydd's engine. Annie began to understand, but was also thinking how this could affect the family. She was beginning to feel angry.

'I was also wondering if we could rescue Jean,' ventured George unwisely. 'We could do with help keeping this house and someone like Jean could be part maid part shop assistant.'

At this Annie's anger doubled.

'So you thought that would help you to jump ship did you? Well we might or we might not be able to help Jean, it's far too early to tell, but it annoys me that you think you can use that poor girl in your plans. And, if I remember rightly, the whole blessed point of the shop was to keep us all employed in the family trade.'

George felt ashamed. This was an unexpectedly strong reaction from Annie and he could think of no defence. If this was what he could expect from the rest of the family he was going to have to keep quiet on the subject for some time. Annie echoed his thoughts.

'I don't think you should mention your plans to anyone else,' she said as she stomped off to prepare the evening meal.

CHAPTER TWENTY-FIVE

'She's seventeen and comes from Staffordshire and was the fifth in a family of eight. An elder brother was injured in a pit accident when he was eleven and while he was recovering he taught himself to read. He encouraged Jean to help him in this so she can read a bit and add up.'

Annie was relating to George and Tillie what Jean had told her of her history when next she had come to buy provisions.

'Her father was a furnaceman and spent a lot of his wages on drink. The family's poverty led to the children leaving as soon as they could. Jean came to London hoping for work in service. Her present position is her second, neither of them happy. She says the jobs that are easy to get are generally miserable, or so she has heard from other women.'

'It sounds like promising children let down by circumstances,' said George. 'There but for the grace of God go we, as they say. Perhaps, Tillie, you could employ Jean part time and she could come and work in the shop, say, some afternoons to get experience. We could pay her a small wage.'

Annie gave George a fierce look. She wasn't going to mention his desire to look for other work, though there was that temptation to spring it on Tillie. She had given George her opinion but realised that her anger wasn't going to change anything so was not going to reject the idea of employing Jean.

'Well, I could do with help around the house,' said Tillie. 'I don't mind the housework; I'm used to it. But I'd like to do something creative, especially if it could earn some money.'

Meanwhile, Jean herself was giving her future some thought. On the day following her emotional visit to the shop she gave in her month's notice. There were many aspects of domestic service she could put up with. The long hours and grinding routine for low wages she accepted but she was not going to be physically abused. She had seen enough of that as she was growing up. A tiny hope sprang up when Annie had taken an interest in her, though she refused to let it grow. So she was astounded when, on her next buying trip to Yeoman's, Tillie was summoned and the proposal that Annie and Tillie had worked out was put to her.

'But where would I be living?'

'You'd have a room in our house,' said Tillie. 'We have to get a bit of furniture for it.'

'An iron bedstead with lumpy mattress – they make them specially for the use of us maids.'

This instance of chirpy humour delighted Tillie, who promised to look out for one. She knew perfectly well that a distance had always to be kept between employer and employee but on her parent's farm this had never ruled out friendship. There was no reason, other than working out her notice, why she shouldn't take on her new role straight away. Given the treatment she had suffered recently, she would hardly expect a good reference from her employer. On balance, however, it was decided that she should continue to the end unless there was another case of physical abuse.

CHAPTER TWENTY-SIX

T he new pattern of working settled to everyone's benefit, though George still entertained hopes to break away to a new career. Dafydd was away for longer shifts as activity on the railways increased and Jean provided pleasant company for Tillie and Lilian, as well as competently working at Yeoman's. The dairy shop, which had been inspired by Dafydd's visit, was soon well established and a dozen small shops followed as the population of the district increased. Notable amongst these was a bakery and a hardware shop.

Into this developing community came news one morning devastating for the Yeomans. It came in the form of Thomas, the youngest of the Yeoman family, arriving breathless in the shop one morning.

'Da's had a collapse,' he gasped. 'Down his right side. Can't move. Hospital.'

Having delivered his fateful message, he went through to the back room and fell onto a chair. George and Annie stared at each other.

'A collapse?'

'Maybe apoplexy,' said Annie. 'It's something to do with blood supply – or lack of it, I think.'

There were no customers in the shop so they went through to the back where Thomas seemed to have recovered his breath.

'Thomas. Was business finished for the day?' asked Annie. Thomas nodded.

'I'll go down, George. See how things are. Thomas can stay here for now.'

Arriving at the family home, Annie was told that Queenie had gone to St Stephen's Hospital, where Victor had been taken. Having ascertained that her two younger siblings were coping with the sudden misfortune, Annie set off for the hospital. Never having been inside one before, she felt daunted by the unfamiliar sights, smells and the unceasing activity she saw. She found a helpful orderly who gave her directions to the admissions area, where she found Queenie alone on a bench.

'Oh Annie, thank goodness. Thank you for coming.' Queenie got up to give her daughter a passionate and relieved hug. 'What a worry. Vic's always been so healthy. Such a shock.'

'How bad is it, and where is he anyway?'

'He's being checked by a doctor. I've got to stay here.'

They sat on the bench and shared their worries and practical concerns.

'I'll stay at the garden for the time being. Jean is doing well when she works in the shop, so George can do without me. Oh, this must be the doctor.'

They both stood and waited with some trepidation as the doctor approached and introduced himself.

'Good morning. I'm Doctor Warren and, it's Queenie isn't it and …'

'My daughter Annie.'

'To put your minds at rest, Victor has suffered only mildly which, as you know, has affected his right side. Such cases can be short lived and we hope this will be the case, but we'll keep him here overnight so we can keep an eye on things.'

'Can we see him?' asked Annie.

'Best to wait for the visiting time. They're quite strict about that,' said Dr Warren.

He smiled and departed. Annie and Queenie made their way to the street after noting the official visiting times. They were both disappointed and slightly aggrieved that they wouldn't see Victor until then.

'Yes it's a pity but at least he's being looked after and the doctor seemed hopeful,' said Annie, relief evident in her voice.

Having reached home they sent Simeon, the middle boy, off to Primrose Hill to give George the news and let him know that Annie would be staying in London. Thomas would return with Simeon later.

CHAPTER TWENTY-SEVEN

'**G**ot to get used to it I suppose,' said Victor grumpily.

Annie sat by his bed, deciding that she did not like hospitals. Smells of boiled cabbage and laundry mingled with vapours from what she presumed were medical substances. It had been strange walking into the ward to look for her father's bed. She had only ever known him as a fit, active man, so it was with an effort that she greeted him as if there was nothing particularly wrong. She spent the first ten minutes of her visit reassuring him that he was far from disabled and that he would still be central to the business. Also that she would be there for the time being to make sure trade was not interrupted. Victor, like many able people suddenly finding their activities limited, was not so sure. Annie did her best to cheer him up until a loud handbell rang to close the visiting hour. As Annie left the ward, Victor felt suddenly lonely.

At Primrose Hill George was worrying. Covent Garden was his father's life and he was going to miss the vigour of their commerce if this illness threatened his mobility. If Annie was going to return to the city for a while it was fortunate that Jean could be in the shop to handle sales when George went out on deliveries. Between drop-offs he tried to work out how the two family businesses would run now. Certainly he would have to forgo any ideas about leaving for the time being. He could imagine Jean becoming a full-time shop assistant but that would be a big step for the family and they would have to discuss the matter, along with all the other permutations. Until now all staff, except Jean herself, who had until now been working on a casual basis, were family members. Not particularly as policy but well, it was a family business. Tillie had helped out in a casual way and Jean's part-time role had in a way followed on from that and there was no doubt that those additions had been useful.

A sudden thought hit George as he plodded along with his handcart. He halted so abruptly that the horse and cart ambling along just behind nearly ran him down.

'Hey, whaty'r up to, boy?' shouted the grizzled driver.

'Sorry, I just had a thought,' called out George who could think of nothing better to say.

'Better leave that to people with brains, chum. Be safer for everyone.'

Seeing that his thought had deprived George of movement, the carter, with much complaining, shuffled around and continued on his way, muttering as he went.

The thought for which George had risked injury was no less than perhaps he should ask Jean to marry him. He stood where he was for several minutes considering the various startling aspects of the thought. The thought in fact had quickly split into a multitude of small thoughts. He felt keenly his lack of romantic experience. There had been various flirtations and fumblings in the nooks of Covent Garden but the only girl he had really wanted to get to know had been Tillie, and he had been too late for her. But wasn't Jean similar in many ways to Tillie? Since coming to help in the shop she had in fact blossomed. She and Tillie shared a sense of humour, though right from the start Jean had been sharper and jauntier. Tillie seemed very fond of her and the two women would often engage in a jousting type of repartee which was on a higher level than that heard at 'the garden'.

It was clear to him now that he had only ever considered Jean as a useful worker who might one day be the means by which he could set off on his own. But Jean was after all an attractive young lady and this new appreciation struck George with such force that he felt a bit dizzy. He was amazed to find, having known Jean for so long as just a casual worker in the shop, that his body quite suddenly felt aroused. Also, worryingly, a mixture of guilt and embarrassment. Am I, he worried, going to start stuttering and blushing next time I meet her?

Realising that he was soon to find out, he tried to prepare a suitable countenance. His efforts were, however unnecessary, as Thomas and Simeon were still present in the shop. They were engaged, together with Jean and Tillie, who had come round with Lilian, in a heated discussion concerning the unexpected change in circumstances. George tried to pick up the subjects, which was difficult at first as they were talking about schools.

'Do you mean some of them want all children to go to school?' asked Jean.

'That's right,' said Tillie. 'And there's a plan to build one round here.'

'But we already go to school,' said Thomas.

'Yes but that's your church school. This is about going to school every day,' said Tillie.

'I don't want to,' said Simeon. 'What about helping at the market?'

'It could be that will change. With railways and ships and factories people will be needed who can do arithmetic and can read. Far more people will be doing apprenticeships in skilled trades. You might want to learn more subjects. Perhaps the family business will have to employ people to keep it going.'

There was silence while each of them contemplated this. Thomas was trying to see the connection between reading and running a railway. George thought it an appropriate moment to break in to the discussion.

'Actually, would you be able to do longer hours for a while, Jean?'

He was relieved that he could speak to Jean about the ordinary matters that needed addressing. Thereby avoiding the danger of getting tongue-tied. Jean looked at Tillie, who frowned then burst out laughing.

'That'll be fine, Jean. I shall miss you, but I haven't forgotten how to look after myself.'

'Good.' George looked at Thomas and Simeon. 'Well I'm going to get these two back home. Come when you can in the morning, Jean.'

He was aware that he had sounded somewhat abrupt but, he reasoned, the circumstances called for firmness.

The three brothers left the shop. Tillie looked round to see what Lilian had been doing.

'Oh, look at that Jean.' She pointed to where Lilian had been quietly occupying herself, building a pyramid out of onions.

Jean went over to inspect the little structure.

'That's beautiful, Lil. What is it?'

'Onions,' said Lilian.

CHAPTER TWENTY-EIGHT

D afydd arrived home to be greeted by an unusual silence. The house was missing the chatter of the three females. The fire in the range was low and the appetising aroma of food cooking was sadly absent. He revived the fire and put the joint from the safe in to roast. There was the usual variety of vegetables on the counter so he started to prepare carrots and potatoes. Soon afterwards his family and Jean arrived at the front door with Lilian in a tearful state.

'Want to stay at the shop,' she wailed.

Dafydd swung the door open and held out his arms. Lilian's tears disappeared at once as she ran forward to be picked up and swung around by her father.

'So, you want to do the night shift at Yeoman's do you? There won't be many customers you know.'

'And not many staff for you to boss around either,' said Jean as she climbed the stairs to her room.

Tillie brought Dafydd up to date with the day's drama, most importantly that Annie had gone into town and might have to stay there for some time. Dafydd listened gravely.

'So some changes for us, perhaps,' he said.

Tillie explained that Jean would be working longer at the shop but that they hadn't yet talked about the details, or how much or little Jean would be giving to her housemaid role. They agreed to see how the situation with Victor developed and in the meantime to free Jean to work at the shop.

'Those two will be spending a bit of time together, I'm thinking. I wonder how they'll get on,' said Dafydd musingly.

Tillie laughed. 'Whatever can you be thinking?'

'Well, why not? Might work out quite well.'

'You can't always arrange peoples' lives you know. Anyway, I shouldn't think George would want to mix business with romance.'

Along the street the subjects of their concern were also thinking about the changes. It had certainly been a strange day with unexpected and unwanted events. George hadn't been able to find out much in town, and returning to the cold shop his thoughts had soon centred on Jean. Jean, who he had regarded in a new light this evening. He wondered how foolish he might prove to be. For all he knew she might already have other possibilities. Later, as he got into his chilly bed, he decided that nothing could be done for the present but at least he could try to find out how Jean regarded him. That settled, he slept well, waking early to concentrate on the new arrangements.

Jean took some time before she slept. She was uneasy. Earlier she had come down to eat with the family then washed up before retiring. There in fact was the problem, she thought. In a way she occupied a position somewhere between a maid and a member of the family. Tillie carried out as much of the domestic work as she herself did and there was no formality in their relationship. She supposed that Tillie's upbringing on a farm accounted for her relaxed attitude and her lack of desire to be waited on. Jean's work in the shop had been a career promotion, but the duality of her life caused her to feel vulnerable. Technically, Tillie could dismiss her at any time. Then what? Jean was not unaware of the fact that she had been rescued from a life of poverty and harshness, but she did not want to feel indebted for ever. She wondered how the new circumstances would affect her. She had grown fond of Tillie, Dafydd and Lilian, and would love to be their friend on a different basis. There was no way of resolving the tangle and sleep eventually overtook her.

CHAPTER TWENTY-NINE

———•———

'I'm going to need you to be working full time.'

George had begun the day with confidence. He had decided to put it to Jean baldly since arrangements had to be made quickly and with firmness. Jean was taken aback with echoes of last night's thinking circulating in her head. She could see that this unexpected statement might simplify her position, but she needed guarantees.

'That would mean becoming a full-time employee with a wage.'

'Perfectly true,' George agreed.

'That would be different to how your family run things. I don't even know how you all arrange payments. And what would happen to me if Victor makes a full recovery, as we hope?'

George had anticipated this question.

'I personally guarantee your position as permanent. We must remember your discussion last night. I'm sure the family will wish the children to attend school if the opportunity arises. Times are changing and family concerns may soon not be relying on family members to work for them.'

The new church clock chimed the half hour and Jean began quickly unlocking and uncovering stock.

'I'll have to talk to Tillie. I don't want to let her down.'

'No, that's good. Anyway, we'll be all right today since there's no delivery from town.'

George was assuming that he would have to take Victor's place on these trips as his father always managed the horse and its fittings and drove the cart. He was hoping that Queenie and Annie could soon manage these duties together.

At ten o'clock Jean went along to help Tillie and let her know what George was proposing. She found Lilian playing a counting game with her mother.

'How many Jeans can you see?'

Lilian giggled. 'One.' She ran over to hold Jean's hand.

Jean began. 'I'm so grateful for everything you've done for me.'

Tillie gave her a sideways glance.

'That sounds like a goodbye.'

Jean explained.

'It was to be expected but I shall miss you. And I don't mean the work. I can sort that out. Just having you around.'

'I was hoping to keep the room,' Jean said tentatively.

'Goodness! Of course you can keep your room. I'll tell you what we'll do. We'll change the room. We'll sublet. It'll no longer be the part time maid's room but a room with a proper tenant. How about that? We'll get those Yeomans to give you a good wage so you can pay us rent. I'll find a part-time daily maid to help me.'

Jean couldn't reply immediately. She was close to tears so just nodded and smiled.

'Thank you so much. I love you both. Better get to the shop before George starts tearing his hair out.'

Lilian looked alarmed. 'Oh, not really, Lil. It's just a saying.'

Tillie called out as Jean disappeared.

'Eat with us tonight, I hope.'

CHAPTER THIRTY
– Extracts from Jean's diary, 1864

January 20

There has been a family tragedy. Victor suffered another and fiercer attack and passed away. The whole Yeoman family are grief stricken. But Victor was almost a stranger to me and I to him because of the way the business is arranged. So I didn't see him much but enough to admire him. He was a hard-working, honest man. But I can't feel sorrow the way the Yeomans and to some extent Tillie, Lilian and Dafydd do. I feel helpless to comfort them and think the best I can do is keep things going here at Primrose Hill. I am alone in the shop as everyone else has gone into town. The heavy snows we had earlier in the month caused shortages and we are low on stock but the customers are coming in as usual. I am telling them what has happened so they won't be surprised if the shop is closed on and off. All this has happened in two days. It is strange. I am now a shop assistant properly. It has more respect than housemaid and better wages, I hope. It is so sudden that nothing has been agreed about my terms or routine. It'll all have to wait 'til things have settled. My diary is a good way of seeing my life change. Also the area. It is fast. The railway pushes it along with the engines and sidings where goods trucks are organised. There is a lot of soot from the engines, which gets everywhere though most winds blow it away from the hill. My last employer got angry when the washing got dirty and I was always to blame. I'm so glad and grateful to be away from that and to be with kind people.

January 27

Victor was buried today. I thought I was to stay in the shop to keep it open. But George wanted me to go to the funeral and said the rest of the family had invited me. It was a very big affair at the church of St Clement Danes, which is near the Covent Garden market and to where the Yeomans have their house. I have never been to such a grand church. They say it is the church in the song, 'Oranges and Lemons'. There was a big crowd, many to do with the market. There were several deaths in our family in Stoke, including a brother of mine and more in other families. But I have never been to a funeral like this. Everything bigger and the church richly furnished. After the service, which was very formal, we followed the hearse in a hired carriage to Tower Hamlets Cemetery. Several people went in cabs so we were about forty for the ceremony and interment. There were many tears as the coffin was lowered and I too felt much distress. My loss was never having the chance to know Victor well. Many of the attenders went on to the family home, some in cabs and some walking, it not being a great distance. George wanted to walk and invited me to accompany him. We walked along in silence, then he offered me his arm which I took, though a bit startled. I must get used to my new station, not a mere housemaid anymore. It has been a strange week for us all but I have noticed that George seems nervous around me. Is he worried about my new role? That has come about through Victor dying. But even so he has been showing me all the ins and outs of the shop workings. Records and ordering and the money side. We said not a word on the way and so reached the house, which I had never been to. It is a large house in a square. I wonder now where the family's wealth comes from, considering they bought the two houses in Primrose Hill. There was plentiful refreshment in the large drawing room. Bread and cold meats and cheeses. Plus a variety of sweet cakes and different fruit juices. Everyone was lively and talkative. I suppose that is how grief is, coming and going all the time, and people needed a change from the sadness of the sombre funeral.

February 12

Things have settled mostly since Victor's funeral. Now I am a shop assistant I will be paid seven shillings a week. I am to pay Dafydd and Tillie two shillings a week rent for the room which they let with the Yeoman's permission. It is a different position to be in, though better than before. I usually share an evening meal with Tillie and Lilian. Dafydd is there sometimes but is often at work. Lil loves me to be there, though sometimes I cook for me and George. I catch him looking at me sometimes but then is embarrassed. I am wondering what he is thinking and could it be that he is considering romance. We are together a lot and get on well but I suppose in the past we just saw ourselves in practical ways. If he does entertain ideas other than that, should I encourage him? What do I want? Maybe to be like Tillie, a family, but I don't want to live in poverty again or make my children live with hunger as I did. Sometime ago Tillie told me, though perhaps she shouldn't have, of the time George visited the farm, not knowing she was engaged, hoping to see her. He is an attractive good-natured man. This area is getting rougher with the railway getting busier. There are plenty of drinking places and the railway men are thirsty. George and Dafydd are happy to drink but keep their wits about them. Dafydd of course has to be careful. There have been reports of engine men being drunk on duty and losing their jobs. The thought of it!

February 22

We can almost see the end of winter. There is more daylight. Although most of our customers are women there are a few young men come in. They are more jaunty now spring is coming and they do give me some attention in a slightly ribald way. I have always been sharp and quick, which they enjoy, and try to get the better of me. They don't do it when George is present but he has heard it going on when in the back room. I wonder what he thinks. Tillie has told me that she'd forgotten how much time the housework takes and has engaged a maid for half days. Til is quite creative and artistic. She often draws flowers and plants and keeps some as pressings. Dafydd brings back samples from his travels. George is still going into London to collect our stock and drive it back here in the cart. The rest of the family are well but we don't see them very often. George goes every Sunday to the family dinner and meeting, so I go then to see Tillie.

March 15

An important event. Dafydd has been promoted to engine driver. He is elated, as is Tillie, and as for Lil she tells all the customers if she's in the shop. My daddy's an engine driver and makes suitable sounds. Well there's plenty to copy. We hear trains all day here. His uplift is earlier than expected. I suppose with the increase in railway activity they will be short of drivers. Some warmer evenings George has invited me for a stroll. Yesterday we walked down to where they have been talking of building a school. It's a field with working horses at the moment near the canal. Is he courting me? I don't know but if so he's taking it slowly. I am very fond of him and could love but I don't want to hope then be disappointed.

March 26

There was a fight last night near one of the public drinking places near the railway. We're told it's getting more common. There are many railway workers but probably a lot more builders. It's strange the different buildings going up. A lot of small houses in terraces for workers but also large houses all over the area, which must be for wealthy people. Dafydd came into the shop and was telling me about his new work as a driver. At first he will be taking engines to the sheds, or what is called shunting wagons. But he says even then it's thrilling to set these huge machines in motion and to feel the power of them. He and George are planning to go rowing soon. Racing each other of course. I know George has been teaching Dafydd swimming. I'm glad of this. In most ways Dafydd is like a brother and because he's quite a bit older it's good that George can be in charge sometimes.

April 12

Dafydd has driven his first passenger train. Well, although he handled the train, there was a more experienced driver with him to advise on the line. They went to Windsor but were passengers on the return. Dafydd brought back a daffodil from Windsor Station to mark his first main line journey. Tillie says she will add it to her pressings. The word in Welsh for leek is the same as for daffodil Dafydd told us, and so they are both used as Welsh symbols. There is to be a ceremony on the twenty-third to mark Shakespeare's three hundredth. George has invited me to go with him. It's a Saturday and he says we will shut the shop a bit early. An oak tree is to be planted at four o'clock. Neither George or I know any Shakespeare so I don't know why he is so keen. He's being mysterious about it.

April 23

What an extraordinary day. George has proposed marriage. It leaves me somewhat breathless. We shut up as planned and walked over to the hill. There were hundreds of people and readings from Shakespeare were taking place, some quite dramatic. People were walking around in Elizabethan costume with much bowing and curtseying. Then there was the planting of the oak tree. I'm not sure if everyone could hear the speech but there was a loud cheering as the tree was planted. Everyone began drifting away and that was when George took my hand as we stood at the side of the path with people walking by and asked if he could kiss me. For some reason I was unable to find my voice so I just looked up at him and nodded. Not wanting to attract attention, we were close only for a few moments but with much feeling. Then, looking straight into my eyes he simply said, 'Will you marry me?' For a few seconds I felt quite faint but then my usual sense of mirth took over. 'After one kiss?' I said – 'Well, probably.' I couldn't stop laughing and then George caught the mood and then for a while we did get some glances. We walked back to the shop in a kind of dream.

April 24

Sunday and our usual visit to St Mark's. Afterwards we went back to Dafydd and Tillie's having told them of our intended marriage. They were so delighted but gave the impression that they had expected it, how I don't know. We prepared a celebration lunch over which we discussed the future, which led to a shock for myself and Tillie when George told us how he'd been thinking of leaving the family business. Dafydd already knew his thoughts about this and so it seems does Annie. It would certainly lead to changes but George assures me that my place as his wife and within Yeoman's is secure. I feel happy and have to take in again the big changes to my life since coming to London and how fortunate I have been. I have only written to my family twice and must tell them the news. I will have to find time to visit them soon.

April 25

I do feel very happy and it is wonderful to have found someone I can love. I do, however, wish I'd have known about his possible plans before agreeing to marry. Not that it would have changed my mind but I was seeing one sort of life when now it might be another. I mustn't mind because marriage is a journey into the unknown and changes ought to be exciting.

May 1

George has gone off to town today and will attend the church his family goes to. He'll go on to their usual Sunday dinner and tell them about us. I do hope they'll approve, especially Annie, who I hope will actually be glad for us and the business.

May 2

No one in George's family objected to our engagement. Annie was even relieved that she can for the time being settle back in the family home. George has been to St Marks to make arrangements for the wedding and the putting up banns. It's all becoming real but unreal at the same time. Knowing each other for a long time through work, then this sudden passion that we both feel. I suppose feelings have been there but kept hidden, though I do remember him looking at me often of late.

May 22

A hot day. After morning service Tillie, Lilian, Dafydd, George and I went over to Regent's Park and hired a rowing boat. A leisurely row around the lake. Many people around the water and in boats enjoying the sunshine. A change for the two men who usually hire fast skiffs, I think they're called, and compete with each other as long as there's space. If there's not enough space they have a game by tying the backs of the boats together and rowing hard in opposite directions. A water version of tug-of-war. We will be married in a month on the twenty-fifth of June. We don't have a lot of time together with the delivery round and George still needing to be in London sometimes. We embrace as I go off to Tillie's and my bed. That's our intimacy. George would go further but I don't want to. As I get into bed I reflect that I won't be sleeping on my own much longer and wonder what it will be like. George seems confident and is constantly affectionate, so I hope for a full life with him. I can't say he isn't romantic. He told me a few days ago that the reason he planned to propose at the Shakespeare gathering was to do with the oak tree planting. The tree as it grew would always remind us. It made me tearful to think of.

June 19

Tillie is pregnant. She felt too nauseous to go to church but we didn't know the reason until we got back. We're all pleased, especially Lilian. All the children she plays with have brothers or sisters and she has felt left out occasionally in this respect. I wonder if I'll ever have children. It's a strange thought for me.

June 20

A big surprise; my brother Luke arrived to visit. He came by train and loved that new experience. I am relieved to hear that all is well with my Stoke family, though I realise that we four here feel more like family to me. Of course he wants to stay for our wedding and to return to Stoke to tell our mother about it. She feels too far removed from us southerners to come. Dafydd tells me that his family missed his marriage to Tillie but for different reasons. Tillie's dad has volunteered to run the shop on Saturday, though her ma is looking forward to being there. I am filled with excitement and nervousness. Tillie has been kind and sensitive. I am inexperienced so her advice on the intimate details of married life is valuable.

June 26

Well here I am, Mrs Yeoman. Everything yesterday was perfect, though the weather was somewhat dramatic. Warm and humid with thunder in the distance and once not so distant. There were more than thirty guests. All the Yeomans, Dafydd, Tillie and Lilian and some old friends from the Covent Garden market. Queenie understandably was emotional, thinking of course of Victor, and shed many tears, as did Tillie's mother. A few valued customers had also been invited, one of whom had made their drawing room available for the refreshments. Tillie's farm had been contracted to provide food and drink and everyone went away satisfied. And so to bed, with us both as anxious as the other which, as is our usual way, reduced us to laughter. Tillie had told me that George would be impatient. They can't help it, she said.

Tillie has told me many things, amongst which is that the physical side of marriage can be enjoyable for women. I didn't know that. Anyway, George kept on apologising, though I don't know why. We both did our best and had fun but we're both beginners. I would say our love life holds promise and I will say this is a man I can come to love deeply.

September 2

After two months of getting used to married life George gives me a surprise, though it shouldn't be. He wants to apply to be a fireman, but not the Dafydd sort but a firefighter. He says something called the London Fire Brigade has been formed recently and is recruiting. He has found out that the eyesight requirements are not as strict as those for locomotive crew, not that his eyesight is that bad that I've noticed. He tells me that Vincent, the brother below him, is keen to work at the shop. I would be doing all the administrative work at least at first. I think about this. What if I start a family? We talk about it all evening. We think that the shop will gradually become less to do immediately with the family, though the Yeomans would keep owning it. He will apply then give Vincent a week to get used to things here. I am glad this is happening because, though we get on well at work, I'm always aware of George's need to try a new job and I will be more a housewife like Tillie.

September 10

Good fortune for George. He has been accepted as a firefighter on a month's trial. I should think he will be made permanent. He's fit and strong with lots of experience with horse-drawn carts. Vincent has enjoyed working the shop with me. I think he's glad to get away from what has been his life 'til now to be somewhere new. He'll be getting to know loads of people on his delivery rounds.

October 13

George has attended his first big fire at some offices in town. Several clerks became trapped and were rescued by members of the crew more experienced and more trained at rescue than George. There have been quite a few incidents before this one so he is gaining practice. A lot of their time is spent training to get used to different emergency situations. It sounds very military, with ranks and drill. George is still a fireman fourth class and will hopefully work his way up the ladder. He looks impressive in his smart serge tunic and brass helmet. I do think about the danger involved, but George is loving it. Off they go, our two men, one to use fire and the other to fight it. We feel winter coming. They have been hard recently so all the growers and farmers on whom we depend are taking care to prepare. Dafydd has been talking about going skating on the lake one winter. I hope the two men can find mutual time off to go together. It sounds fun.

CHAPTER THIRTY-ONE
– Extracts from Jean's diary, 1865

January 12

An amazing amount of snow has fallen and it's impossible to get around very far. We can keep the shop open of course because we live on and near the premises, but we're unlikely to get any stock. Lilian thinks it's wonderful and stays out for as long as she can. We have plenty of kindling and coal so can keep warm and fed. The cold is not as bad as those clear frosty days and nights but unpleasant when we try to clear outside the shop and get snow in our clothes and boots. Dafydd and George have gone off to try to get to work but we who are left at home have no idea how they'll get on.

January 13

Our two men eventually returned very late last night. There were no trains running but Dafydd was called on with others who had made it to clear the outside platforms and service roads. George was similarly involved in the streets of London but they were also called to two domestic fires – I suppose they're more likely in this weather. No one was hurt but the delay in getting to the places meant they couldn't save anything of the buildings.

March 12

Tillie's baby decided to arrive in the middle of the night. Her midwife was staying overnight in case this occurred. George and I were both called in to help, so a tired but happy start to the week. All is well and Lilian has a brother. She had made up her mind to be pleased boy or girl and has held to that and is now planning what sort of games she'll play with him!

March 25

There is no sign yet of a baby for George and me, and although the birth of Tillie's second gave rise to a sort of longing, I won't be looking forward to the sleepless nights involved if we are blessed. Meanwhile we have received two pineapples in the latest delivery. I've never seen one before nor have most of our customers. Not that many of them could afford to buy one. There is an increasing amount of stock coming from town that has been brought into the docks from all over the world. Buying such items is risky since they can deteriorate quickly. It's only the better off customers who can afford the lemons, oranges and such like anyway, and few even of them would be able to buy the pineapples.

September 8

I have arranged to visit my family next week. Annie is going to join Vince in the shop for the few days I'll be away. I'm quite nervous about being with family again. I'm not the person I was. I must thank Luke, although it was a few years ago, for helping me to read and write. It was one good thing that came from his accident that we both learned basic letters and numbers. I may not have been rescued by the Yeomans otherwise and I couldn't have kept this diary every day for the past year or so. I don't think I gave Luke enough attention when he visited because of my wedding, so hope to make amends.

September 13

I'm very glad to be back home. Primrose Hill is home more than Stoke ever was. Very strange going back there. Luke has moved out so Mum and the younger ones keep the home going. Dad is still working and drinks less. Maybe he got bored with it. He's more sombre as well as more sober. I must seem very different to them now. Confident and healthy. Mum and Dad are actually wary of me as though I've become a posh southerner. Much easier with Luke, and feel I made up for neglect when he came down. He's doing well as an apprentice in an engineering company.

December 28

What a pleasant Christmas! We shut the shop at eleven on Christmas morning and George drove myself, Tillie with Lilian and Owen to the Hopkins farm for a big afternoon meal. George had to go in to work – fires don't stop for Christmas – and Dafydd had to leave early. We stayed overnight so that we could all be together next day when the two men had most of the day off. More food and the Hopkins cider. Many were the games that Lilian organised for us. She can be quite bossy but not unreasonable. We resolved that the family should spend more time together.

CHAPTER THIRTY-TWO

On 14 January 1867 in Regents Park about twenty people were in
danger when the ice on which they were skating began to break
up. They were rescued by the skating club stewards, known as 'ice men'.

15 JANUARY 1867

Dafydd and George, having unusually coordinated their shifts, set off
with Tillie, Lilian and Owen across the flat snow-covered reaches of
Regent's Park. Their reward would be the delights of the frozen lake.
When she wasn't dancing in the snow, Lilian sat on a homemade sledge
to be pulled along by George or Dafydd. Snowflakes drifted in the air,
prompting Lilian to devise a game.

'Mummy, you can count up to twenty can't you?'

Tillie smiled. 'I'll try.'

'You two see how many snowflakes you can catch on your tongues
before twenty. Starting now.'

Lilian ran in large circles, mouth wide and tongue out.

George and Dafydd joined in and after a count of twenty George
owned to eleven. Dafydd immediately countered, claiming twelve.
Lilian looked dismayed and searched the two men's faces.

'I think you're both telling fibs,' she cried angrily. 'I'm being honest
and I only caught three.'

George tried to look shamefaced. 'Actually I only got one,' he said,
looking at the floor.

'And I missed them all,' Dafydd groaned. 'They just didn't come
near me.'

'Then I win, hooray. I thought I would.'

Lilian grabbed the pulling rope and ran off towards the lake towing
the sledge.

There were hundreds of people on and around the lake, and as they approached Tillie was disturbed by several notices that had been put up at intervals with details of the previous day's incident.

'Did you know about that?' she asked Dafydd, looking also at George.

Apparently neither of them had heard about it and Tillie turned her attention to the large numbers out on the ice.

'Do you think it's safe now?' she asked of both men.

'I hope so. I wouldn't like to think I bought these for nothing.'

Dafydd drew out a heavy pair of skates from the bag he'd been carrying. He began fastening one over a shoe. George took the other one and examined it. He'd never held one before and was interested in the way it had been put together.

'Look over there,' said Dafydd. 'You can hire a pair. How about it?'

George returned the second skate.

'I think I'll wait a bit. I might make a fool of myself.'

'That's probably what I'll do,' said Dafydd, strapping on the other skate.

'Anyway you can see a lot of them don't have skates. They're just sliding around.'

'That's what I want to do. Can I go, Mummy?' asked Lilian.

Tillie looked at Dafydd, who took Lilian's hand.

'Just a little way then. Come on. You can help me to stay upright.'

Tillie and George watched them edge down to the lake shore. The light snow that had been falling covered the surface of the ice and formed changing patterns as skaters and sliders traversed it. Dafydd was tottering slightly with Lilian, giving what support she could. He had to let go of Lilian's hand so that he could wave both arms in the air to keep balance as he took tentative steps along the ice. George and Tillie had to laugh at his antics but they could see he was gaining confidence. So much so that he was soon almost skating in a halting way. Lilian was thrilled to be out on the ice and followed her father with short runs and slides. The lake shore was crowded and a gay fair-like feeling prevailed. People were going out onto the lake as others were returning to rest. Various stalls had been set up, including vendors of roasted chestnuts. George walked over to buy a packet of these while Tillie sat on their sledge, upended to provide a convenient seat. Owen was just waking from a long comfortable sleep in Tillie's sling. It wasn't practical for the two of them to go onto the ice and George was content to keep them company. Tillie was concerned that Dafydd and Lilian were getting further from the shore than she would have liked but though she called to them there was no chance of attracting their attention over the general hubbub.

When George looked back at the event his most vivid memory was the moment of quiet that followed the first loud crack as the ice gave way right across the lake. Almost a vast intake of breath. Immediately after came a crescendo of screams as several hundred people were plunged into the water and others tried to keep their balance on sections not yet fractured. Those near the edge were able to scramble ashore but as the ice sheet fell apart, the weight of many skaters on smaller pieces caused these to break up or overturn.

Watchers round the lake were mesmerised for some seconds as they tried to take in the scale of the disaster unfolding in front of them, then broke into frantic activity as they tried to reach out to the nearest victims. Collectively, some people managed to tear down branches from nearby trees while others ran to the boat moorings and began to fight their way through the shards of ice using heavy oars.

Tillie struggled to her feet and took a step forwards but George grabbed her arm firmly, never once taking his eyes from the spot where he had last seen Lilian. He stripped off his overcoat and ran towards the lake, halting at the edge to get a last glimpse of the girl who had suddenly become more important than life. She was still afloat; he could see her red bonnet. She must be supported by air in her clothing, thought George, but he knew that would soon fail. He leaped into a fissure stretching out from the shore and began to swim and push his way to where he guessed Lilian might be. Plates of ice hit his body, pushed by those still desperately struggling. Several times hands reached out to grip his arms or legs and he violently shook them off. As he struggled on, the thought of Dafydd occurred to him. Dafydd, whom he had taught to swim and who would have to use that ability now to survive. George felt a moment of despair as he thought of Dafydd's heavy skates and clothing. His thoughts returned to Lilian. He reached the point where, looking back to the shore, he judged Lilian must be. There was no sign of her. Warding off feelings of panic and hopelessness he realised that his only chance was to go under and rely on Lilian's partial buoyancy to prevent her sinking too far. He dropped below the surface and began to swim as fast as he could in zigzags, occasionally opening his eyes to get a very blurred and restricted view of the surroundings. By feel alone he would have missed her but just after his

114

third emergence for breath he dived again and caught sight of a leg and foot clearly belonging to a child. Two fierce strokes brought him within reach and he prayed as never before that the child was Lilian. Other children had been on the lake and George knew that if this was one such, he would be bound to rescue him or her and Lilian would die. It needed all his strength and swimming skill to push himself and the body the two feet to the surface. As he glimpsed the face through her swirling hair the feeling of relief he experienced almost caused a faintness. He had Lilian, but why wasn't she conscious, and was she alive? George began the battle to get back to the shore with one arm flailing water and pushing large lumps of ice out of the way and the other holding tightly around Lilian's body. He knew he'd reached the edge of the lake when he felt Lilian's body being pulled from his grasp.

The shouted instruction, 'Let go, we've got her,' reassured him and she was gone. Immediately he felt strong arms dragging him up the grassy bank. He lay still, eyes closed, dizzy with exertion and cold. Other people were attending to Lilian now and the desire to know her fate was countered by the dread of being given bad news. He turned over and raised himself but was unable to see past the knot of people around Lilian and Tillie. They were still and hushed as he watched, but then a loud cheer and relieved laughter erupted and several from the group turned to look at him. One man cried, 'This fellow's a hero. He saved that young girl's life.' There was applause and smiles as they surrounded him. George struggled to his feet. Seeing that he was making his way towards Lilian and Tillie, several people came over to help. George saw that Lilian had been wrapped in his discarded coat and Tillie was doing her best to hold her in a firm embrace. He noticed that someone else was holding Owen. Tillie was persuaded to give Lilian up to willing hands of volunteers, who attempted to give her some warmth. All those involved along the bank were moving towards the park's exits. It was clear that survivors needed to be taken somewhere for treatment, warmth and clothing. The lake itself had become ominously quiet. George edged close to Tillie, who met his eyes with a pleading look that made him oblivious of his own discomfort.

'Where's Dafydd? Did he get away?' she sobbed.

George was at a loss for an answer. He didn't know for certain what had happened to Dafydd or anyone else and he wasn't going to give Tillie false hope. He remembered his thoughts as he forced his way through the ice and, since Dafydd had been close to Lilian when the ice gave way, he wasn't hopeful. In the end he murmured that they would just have to wait, though he could see that this was the very thing that was going to be agonising.

News of the disaster was spreading quickly, and around the park there were scenes of growing activity. Cabs had been summoned and private vehicles were coming to the rescue of the many soaked and freezing survivors. Somehow George and Tillie were bundled with Lilian and Owen into a carriage that took them to a house in Bayswater, where they were quickly rushed into a large room where a bath was being filled with hot water. Lilian was undressed and put into the bath as soon as a suitable temperature was reached. She had been trembling violently; cold and shock playing their parts. George was shivering for the same reasons and was persuaded to surrender his clothes and enter the hot water as soon as Lilian had reached a normal temperature. The drawing room was crowded with members of their host family and domestic staff. There was great curiosity about the accident but no questions were asked until Lilian and George were warm and dry and dressed in a variety of clothes. Tillie sat, tearful, on a dining chair that had been brought in. George took the dominant woman who was obviously the mistress of the house aside and told her about Dafydd, and asked her to impart the knowledge discreetly to everyone present. He then gave an account of the accident and, though it was the last thing he wanted to do, the kindness shown by this household called for an explanation of the afternoon's events. A room was prepared for Tillie and her children since there was no question of them travelling anywhere. George explained that he needed to return home immediately to let Jean know what had happened. He set off in his borrowed clothes with the assurance that his own would be ready for him the next day. As he left the house he had the presence of mind to note the street name and house number as a precaution. His mind was in such confusion that he wasn't sure he'd remember the way the next day.

Some sort of news had preceded George so that when he arrived home he found Jean in a state of extreme anxiety. She greeted him with a long passionate embrace, expressing her relief at his arrival. Though she was desperate to know what had happened, George for some time could not speak at all. Emotions, suppressed for hours, overwhelmed him, and leaning against a wall he cried bitterly. Jean had never seen

George in tears and the fears that sprung up in her mind frightened her. She carried a chair over and gently drew George to sit down. She cradled his head and waited. As soon as he could George began an account as he remembered it.

'I was standing with Tillie on the banks of the lake. Dafyyd had put on his skates and gone out onto the ice with Lilian. They stayed near each other as Dafydd tried to skate. Lilian just slid up and down enjoying herself. There was a sharp sound and the ice broke across the lake. Big areas of it tilted then they broke up. There were too many people out there. The weight was too much.'

George stopped and gathered himself to go on.

'A lot of people were able to scramble across the larger sections to the bank but the rest fell into the water. I had been watching Lilian and tried to keep my eyes on her. She floated for a while and I was able to rescue her.'

'You went into the lake?' Jean was amazed.

'There was no other way. I was lucky to find her.'

A question hung in the ensuing silence.

'And Dafydd?'

She hadn't wanted to ask and was afraid of the reply. George breathed deeply.

'I really don't know. Everything was so confused and I hardly knew where I was after being in the water.'

Jean was glad not to hear definite news, though she sensed that George was not hopeful. She shuddered. How was Tillie going to cope if she lost her husband?

George continued his narrative, describing their journey to the large house, followed by getting warm again. He would be going there tomorrow, he said, and would get a picture of what had happened. Jean had already prepared a meal and despite George's distress he found that he was hungry enough to eat.

'When I first heard I didn't know what to do. Whether to come to the park or stay here,' said Jean.

'You did the right thing and I'm glad you did. If you'd gone over there we would never have met up today.'

George slowly climbed the stairs. He slept long and deeply and thankfully, escaped, if briefly, from sorrow.

CHAPTER THIRTY-THREE
– Extracts from Jean's Diary, 1867

January 17

This must be life at its darkest. Tillie is in the deepest of grief and we are all mourning the loss of Dafydd. Still ahead of us is the request to identify his body, since they haven't all been recovered. We have heard that divers are employed to search the lake. It must be a horrible job. George spent most of yesterday chasing around all the places that survivors had gone to, keeping alive the faint hope for Tillie that Dafydd lived, but he knew it was useless. He had been watching Dafydd and Lilian and knew they were close together when the ice broke and if Dafydd had managed to get to land we would have known. We have kept the shop open. People must have their food. Many of our customers have been coming to express their sorrow, making me realise that a strong community has built up in the area over years. The newspapers have given a lot of space to the accident, even including drawings put together by artists. Lilian has recovered but I don't think has fully recognised the loss of her daddy. She has no memory of what happened to her, just stepping out on the ice. She has a bruise on her head and we think she may have been hit by a lump of ice and that may have saved her if it prevented her taking gulps of air and water. Tillie's mother arrived this afternoon and will stay for the time being. So, with us, Tillie has love and support.

January 19

All hope was lost when Tillie went to identify Dafydd's body, but I suppose that's when the loss becomes definite and true mourning can take place. Oh, we had such a happy family; why did they have to go skating? And why wasn't I with them? Not that it would have made any difference if I'd shut the shop and gone. We have sent a letter to Dafydd's family. What terrible news to get in a letter, even if they weren't on good terms. Tillie is being a good mother but of course cries her heart out in private. Lilian is old enough to accept facts. A younger child might keep asking when Daddy was coming home. Our routines continue day to day but it's hard. The weather is harsh and supplies to the shop are restricted to basic vegetables. George is making the funeral arrangements. Dafydd will be buried at Highgate Cemetery. I asked George whether the railway company had been told, but of course he had done that in between searching among survivors. I'm wondering whether Tillie will get any sort of pension, but dare not ask at the moment.

March 25

It is so good to be leaving winter behind. When I feel the sun and see the spring flowers and buds bursting I realise that life overcomes death. The only time Tillie cries passionately now is when she looks at the daffodils. She remembers the one Dafydd brought her on the day of his first engine drive. Owen shows no sign of distress, we thank God. George has been especially important to Lilian and he hides the pain he feels at the loss of his close friend. Several times Tillie has asked me to walk over to the lake with her, which I do, and I know she goes sometimes on her own. I really do not know what thoughts she has but she will stand there gazing out over the water for a time, either gently weeping or, amazingly, faintly smiling. She has said that she might go back to live at her parents' farm. If she and the children do go, we must be prepared for our hearts to be broken once again.

CHAPTER THIRTY-FOUR
– Gloucester

———•————

'I've found something I'd love to see, if we can get tickets.' A delighted Julie was holding a magazine that listed events in London. 'It's called Pacific Overtures, composed by Stephen Sondheim. Have you heard anything by him. I really love his work.'

'I'm not sure if I have. Tell me one or two.'

'Well possibly the most well known isn't the score at all; just the lyrics. That's for the West Side Story musical. The music was by Leonard Bernstein.'

'Yes well I've seen the film and the words and music are wonderful, and everyone knows some of them, but what's this Pacific one about?' enquired Peter, his look slightly more anxious than usual. He knew he'd be out of his depth with music of any sort.

'It's about the history of Japan. How it was discovered and exploited by the West,' said Julie.

'Sounds more like a lecture than a musical,' said Peter. 'What a strange subject to choose.'

Julie laughed. 'That's nothing. Another musical he composed is about Sweeney Todd; you know, the so-called "Demon Barber of Fleet Street". He cut people's throats and they were made into pies!'

'I think I'd prefer Japan,' chuckled Peter. 'I'll try to get tickets. Lend me that magazine with the details.'

Peter was still feeling remiss regarding his supposed scepticism, so to compensate booked train tickets and a hotel for the night as well as for the show. Julie's ideas had strayed a long way from those he would normally allow within the Science Group. They were edging too close to what many would classify as paranormal. He refused to use that word on the grounds that if phenomena actually existed then they surely counted as normal and open to investigation. It was always possible that the human mind, whether dependent or not on the brain, could operate in ways not easily quantifiable. Particularly if conditions of emotion and other subjective feelings had to be met. Julie was happy to accept his offering, but maintaining objectivity without upsetting her looked like being a bit of a balancing act.

A sharp east wind greeted them as they set out for London. Only April could provide such a day. Spells of hot sunshine alternating with cold gusts and snow flurries. Conditions were the same in London and added excitement to their short walk from Paddington Station to Regents Park. Julie's eagerness to get to the park precluded a coffee stop, to Peter's disappointment, though he understood her impatience. She had been reading everything she could about the lake tragedy and now to be so near the actual location ruled out any delay.

On first sight of the lake Julie stopped and gazed for a short while, taking it in. Peter wondered what she was thinking but knew not to ask. They had to walk along the shore and cross a bridge to reach the place Julie thought corresponded to her dream. She avoided looking at the water as they approached the spot, then stood with her back to the lake before turning to face it. If she expected an immediate revelation of any kind she was disappointed, but was prepared to wait. Certainly the scene before her looked familiar, but that would be expected after the artist's impressions she had studied. As Peter watched, a puzzled look came over her face.

'What is the feeling?' he asked.

Julie didn't answer immediately but continued to look perplexed.

'Not at all what I may have imagined. But strange. Do you ever get those fleeting memories right out of the blue. A place, something you did. Quite ordinary but nothing to have triggered them?'

'Yes. I've had moments like that, but I've never looked into it.'

Julie paused, concentrating.

'Well when I turned to look at the lake I got several, one after the other. Not pleasant or unpleasant but somehow annoying. They're fading now. But definitely my memories. How peculiar.'

She suddenly laughed and looked almost pleadingly at Peter's face.

'What do you make of it?' she said.

Peter was intrigued. It was, as Julie had said, not what one would have imagined or expected. He searched for an answer.

'Did any of these memories relate to ice or lakes or disasters?'

'Not that I could say. No, not at all.'

'But they were memories and you could say that being here, on this spot, had something to do with it,' said Peter.

Julie agreed but resolved to have a chat with Paul about his crash site visit. He'd never described any feelings at the site or after the visit but he may have considered that any random memories were irrelevant and not worth mentioning. They decided to put aside the mystery, if mystery there was, for the time being.

'Before we go, though, could I ask a favour? I want to spend a few minutes here on my own. Perhaps you could wait at the bridge for me.'

Peter readily agreed and trotted off. He knew there was a three-mile road circuit around the park and he longed to run it three or four times, but unfortunately this was not included in the day's plan. His new relationship with Julie had led to a decrease in his weekly mileage and he was feeling the deprivation.

Julie stood and gazed out over the lake. The boat-hire business had opened and a few hardy rowers were exercising vigorously. So this was where it had happened. The fun and happiness on a winter's day shattered with the ice. Was there really any connection between that and herself? Did a distant relative stand on this spot, helpless and horrified? Perhaps today was all that was needed to lay the ghost to rest. As she watched, the sparkling wavelets darkened as a heavy cloud brought a flurry of snow. The water would still be cold at this time of year. But in January! She shivered. But what if something more was required of her. A sudden thought, daring and dangerous, arrived from nowhere. Suppose that she could go out on the ice one day? The danger need not be too great, as the lake had been made much shallower since 1867. Then it had been twelve feet deep, more than three and a half metres. Now it was supposed to be less than five feet, one and a half metres. She was taller than that.

'Hey, what am I thinking about?' she addressed a passing swan. After today it will all be just a bit of history. She turned and set off at a run to catch up with Peter. Still, surely there could be no harm in tracing her family history. Just for fun. Just to see.

The rest of the day was devoted to visits to the Science Museum, the New Tate Gallery with lunch in between. The Donmar Warehouse was their last destination, where Peter, against any expectation, enjoyed the musical.

'It's amazing the humour Sondheim puts into it.'

'That's one of his talents,' said Julie. 'In Sweeney Todd, he first meets, or reunites with, Mrs Lovett in her pie shop after a long absence, where she admits that hers are the worst pies in London and blames it on the price and scarcity of meat. A harbinger of later events.'

Julie avoided all mention of the lake for the rest of the weekend. which pleased Peter. It wasn't that he lacked interest, but he was hoping that Julie wasn't going to become obsessed. Julie shared the hope, though the faint but persistent pull towards something as yet unknown worried her.

CHAPTER THIRTY-FIVE

———•◆•———

The summer term began in a blaze of hot weather. It was difficult to imagine ice except as a palliative, but, against her own wishes, Julie felt herself drawn further into the lake tragedy. She began to feel the sort of apprehension she might feel just on the edge of a great whirlpool, and a whirlpool meant obsession. There were several obsessions in her past, for which she had resorted to counselling. She had not told Peter of these yet. Had she done so he would probably have noticed early signs. But, she reasoned, here was an interesting mystery that she wished to investigate. Therefore, so long as she kept a sense of proportion, she should be safe. So began the tentative searches of past family, though she soon realised that this was going to take more time and effort than she'd expected. Her father had died and she was reluctant to seek information from her mother, who would want to know in detail her reasons. Not for the first time Julie wondered if her obsessive nature came from her mother's genes.

Her relationship with Peter was now widely known by anyone interested, so Julie didn't resume her visits to the Science Group, thus avoiding embarrassment to either themselves or the students. The exception was during the second week of term when she went along as the members arrived in order to catch Paul. He knew about Julie's early childhood dream and understood her desire to discover its significance. She quickly told him of the visit to the lake but not of her strange, seemingly random memory flashes.

'Paul, you remember that moment on our trip to the crash site when you got out of the car to walk over to the hedge.' Paul nodded, wondering what was coming. 'Was there anything unusual at all that you experienced then, no matter how small?'

Paul tried to recall the scene and yes, there was something that might be odd.

'There was a faint smell of linseed. I assumed it had something to do with the farm so I didn't bother to mention it. I recognised the smell from oiling my cricket bat.'

Julie knew the smell of linseed and certainly would have identified it on the day. But had she noticed it then and since forgotten?

'I was too interested in being there to think it important. Was it? Important I mean,' asked Paul.

'Perhaps not. I don't know. Thanks anyway. Have a good science evening.'

Not much to go on, thought Julie. I wonder if Paul's mum noticed a smell. I really can't go and ask her. I have to be careful that people don't start questioning my sanity. But if there was no smell outside Paul's perception then it could be significant, being in a way relating to memory. But cricket bats!

Next day, being Friday, Peter and Julie cooked a meal together at Julie's. Over the meal, Julie related her conversation with Paul.

'As you say, there's no great revelation and it's a pity Paul didn't say something at the time. That could have been important, but we can't blame him for that. Only ...' Peter paused.

'What?'

'Well, had the smell been real, wouldn't you or his mother have remarked on it?'

Julie sighed. 'The trouble is that the three of us were immersed in this plane accident. That could explain why we didn't. Like Paul, we could have easily put it down to something to do with the farm. We'd only just arrived. Funny though that whereas we don't remember, Paul does. Do you think I should ask his mum?'

'I think it would be in order. Just say the Science Group is doing a bit of research to do with memory. I want to think about what you've told me. We could talk about it on our outing tomorrow.'

The heatwave was over and, with a dry weekend in prospect, Peter had proposed that they visit a site between the Sharpness Canal and the River Severn where, long ago, the hulks of various vessels had been deliberately beached on the east bank of the river to protect the canal. Peter was familiar with the place and never tired of going down to the Severn. He was looking forward to introducing the wrecks to Julie.

CHAPTER THIRTY-SIX

'W ow, what an amazing place.' Julie's amazement grew as they progressed along the footpath that ran parallel to the River Severn.

'I didn't expect such a variety of, what shall we say, vessels.'

'Bits and pieces have disappeared over the years, especially from the timber ships. But they are supposed to be protected now and the Friends of Purton keep an eye on them. They're the ones who researched the information on the plaques you can see.'

'The boats did what they were supposed to do, I should think, so the bank and canal are safe now,' said Julie.

'Yes, and further along you'll see some of them were completely involved. They've been buried in silt and only a plaque remains to show where they were beached.'

'These concrete ones'll last for centuries. I didn't know any boats could be made from concrete,' said Julie.

They reached the last few sites which, as Peter said, were marked only with plaques. A cemetery for these once living working ships. Peter pointed to the place a little further downstream where there had once been a railway bridge used mainly for the transport of coal. He explained how it had been damaged, never to be repaired, by a collision with two small ships carrying explosives.

'At low tides you can still see those vessels. They were never recovered from the river bed. No luck today though as they're well submerged.'

They walked slowly back, hand in hand where the width of the path permitted. Julie stopped and gazed at a long wooden hull far back from the river.

'This is my favourite. "Harriett" with a double "T". I wonder if there was a real woman.'

'I expect so, but I know the plaque doesn't tell you.'

They walked over to read the details.

'Honeystreet. She was built in Honeystreet. What a lovely name. I would like to live there just for that.'

Peter began tapping on his phone.

'It's in Wiltshire. Bit too far to commute I should think.'

'There are other schools. Don't worry,' Julie laughed, seeing a flicker cross Peter's countenance, 'I wouldn't leave you for such a small thing.' She put her arms around Peter and hugged tight. 'Perhaps I'd better rephrase that! How about, I wouldn't leave you for the world?'

But even as she smiled and reassured him she knew of shadows in her personality that could threaten any relationship given time.

They sat resting their backs against the sun-warmed hull of Harriett and each unpacked the food they had prepared to share.

Peter felt the overwhelming sense of peace that he always felt here. The wide, quiet panorama of the Severn stretched out against a backdrop of the Forest of Dean. The railway line to Chepstow ran along the west bank. As they watched, a three-carriage train crawled southwards, rendered tiny and strangely silent by the distance across the river.

'So. Memories,' announced Peter.

'I've been thinking about it a lot and the more I think the more frustrated I get,' said Julie. 'All this mystery about consciousness and dreams, imagination and memory. They're right in front of our noses but it seems we can't get to them in a normal scientific way.' Julie looked almost pleadingly at Peter. 'Do you feel like that?'

'Absolutely. I more and more think that we can't expect to find out about these things using normal methods. There may be intelligence underlying everything and that might make the universe alive and unpredictable. Can you imagine nothingness?' Julie was startled by the unexpected question but Peter went on. 'No time, no space, no dimensions. Nothing.'

Julie put down her fork, frowning. She started to answer then stopped, concentrating.

'But doesn't that pose the question of why does anything exist. Ever?' She finally answered.

'Yes, and I often get a sort of brain vertigo pondering it,' said Peter.

'Is this related in any way to memory?'

'I don't know. Maybe, but I've no idea how.' Peter was beginning to wish he'd not started on this and tried to return to the subject they'd agreed to discuss. 'But your experience, if the reality of it could be verified, would be startling. And the trouble is we could never prove anything because there's nothing to isolate and repeat.'

'But we ourselves might be convinced,' said Julie, hopefully. 'Or one of us.'

Peter smiled. He was not going to be drawn into a discussion about premature positions. He would like to have enough information to be able to formulate at least a hypothesis.

Julie also now accepted a truce on this issue and knew that if she didn't, she herself would start to feel annoyed. The last thing she wanted today. She began a new topic.

'One of the things I've found interesting is that although smells and scents prompt powerful and emotional memories, the memories themselves are generalised rather than specific recollections. For me anyway. So a flower scent might trigger memories of visits to a glasshouse in Kew Gardens but they are vague images without any tags of time or date. But it can be possible to recall a particular visit if something unusual occurred. Like unexpectedly meeting an old friend, or dashing into the glasshouse to shelter from a thunderstorm.'

'That's certainly true for me,' said Peter. 'Perhaps we can say it's related to the associative quality of memory. If I say the word "honey" you might get a vision of bees but not a specific event. But you'd be sure to remember being stung by bees. One of the techniques to remember things is the use of association.'

'Different types of amnesia are surely worth looking at if we are asking whether memories are held within the brain or not,' suggested Julie.

'Vital I should think. It's interesting that the events that may have caused the early images for you and Paul were sudden and violent. Such events can often cause the people involved to suffer amnesia, often to the extent that they cannot recall what happened.'

Julie laughed suddenly.

'So we may have come across someone's lost memories.'

'It may sound humorous, but when you think about it the repetitive dream experiences for both of you didn't relate directly to an event. I mean, they weren't images of the accidents,' said Peter.

'That's right. They were images that could have been peripheral in some way. Paul's could have been a plane waiting to take off. Mine maybe a survivor or loved one at the location. The feelings were different too. Paul felt anxious whereas I felt sorrow and loss. And Paul doesn't seem to feel much present involvement, having now visited the site, but I feel almost as if I was called on to do something.'

Julie was gazing downstream, imagining the steady widening of the Severn as it ebbed and flowed with the ocean. Peter was unsure how to respond to her musing, which he found unsettling.

'How could that be?' he eventually asked.

Julie came back to the moment.

'Oh Peter, we're talking here about things we have little understanding of. But a person can be called on in all sorts of ways. You might be called to go volunteering after reading about people, or animals even, in trouble. Loads of people say they've been called by God. Who are we to gainsay them? And in the cases of Paul and myself, things might be quite different for each of us. One dream might be just an echo; a "don't forget me" type of thing whereas another might be like a request to do something.'

'I've no wish to gainsay anyone's belief that callings originate outside their brains or minds, but there's the difficulty. How do we tell the difference between such calls and those we have formed from our own experiences?'

Julie shrugged and laughed. 'Next question.'

'OK, researchers tell us that the area around the hippocampus is involved in forming memories. Well, does that apply to so-called implanted memories. Those we are told can be formed by suggestion?' asked Peter.

'No reason why not, that I can think of, for what that's worth. But it would seem your imagination would play a big part if a memory is created of, say, an event that had never happened,' said Julie.

'Sure, and where does the imagination lurk? One of the frustrations is that even if you identify an area of the brain that is active for this or that, we still don't know exactly what is happening and we still wonder where this mind is that can access and consider memories.'

Julie felt there was nowhere left to go with this discussion at the moment. She stood and stepped back, taking in the graceful lines of the boat. How wonderful it is that we do have imagination, she thought. She pictured the boatyard in Honeystreet as Harriett had taken shape from day to day. There would be no powered hand tools, so the sounds you would hear would be the gentle swish as boards were planed say, or pegs were hammered in. Her idea of the yard became more vivid. There, an apprentice sweeping up shavings, perhaps to burn in a brazier in winter. Here, the skilled craftsmen working bare chested in the heat of summer. And after several months of toil the barge is ready to take to the water. Would there be a ceremony of any kind? Surely something to mark the beginning of the vessel's life? The men watch with satisfaction as she is drawn into the quay. They turn to prepare for the next order.

Julie walked over to stroke the weather-worn timbers, thinking of the men who had shaped them, all long gone. She suddenly felt the need for action.

'Hey, I think I'm needed on deck,' she shouted, alarming Peter, who watched as she sprinted to the large concrete hulk that lay next in line but nearer to the river.

Using the hand and foothold available she was soon on board. This vessel was frequently lapped by the higher tides and Julie was soon at the further end looking down at the mud below.

'Do not jump into that mud,' shouted Peter. 'It will be quite deep.'

'Yes, sir. Not in the mud. Yes, sir.' Julie saluted and made her way back up the deck.

Peter was relieved. Their discussion hadn't covered half of what he'd wanted but at least he wasn't going to have to rescue Julie from danger. This time.

CHAPTER THIRTY-SEVEN

It might have been just a school orchestra but by the end of the evening Peter was wishing he'd started going to classical concerts earlier in life. He was feeling grateful to Julie for opening up this experience. Vibrations had until now been subjects of scientific study, but this evening they had touched his emotions.

'I tried focusing on you to see if I could actually hear you playing.'

'Well I hope you couldn't because it would probably mean I wasn't in tune.'

Peter assured her that the violins sounded wonderfully together and thanked Julie for inviting him. Julie was in fact pleased with the way she'd played, and this led to her wanting to jump into bed the minute they got back home and Peter, with the sounds of the orchestra fresh in his mind, was no less enthusiastic. They agreed to put post-concert refreshments on hold and, with music clearly playing its role as the food of love, enjoyed a session of inspired love making. As they cooled with Julie stroking, as she loved to do, his lean runner's body, Peter was surprised when she returned to the conversation they'd had at the river a few days before.

'I've been putting together things you've said.'

Peter was reluctant to be brought back to earth but as long as her caresses continued he was content to listen to her latest ideas. He turned onto his front and Julie knelt so that she could apply the long firm strokes up and down his back that she knew he enjoyed.

'It's that you've often said that for phenomena like telepathy or clairvoyance, we would need to know the conditions necessary for these to occur if we are to have any chance of understanding them or even controlling them. So perhaps violent events, possibly but not necessarily linked to amnesia, could lead to the occurrence of such happenings. And maybe these conditions are rare.'

Julie's suggestions seemed totally credible, but the only way Peter could think of pursuing them was by collecting reports and anecdotal material.

'At the risk of sounding spurious, we can't go staging plane crashes or drowning people in lakes to continue our research,' he said.

'Why ever not? That's nothing to what goes on all over the world every day and that's just people trying to get other people to think differently, if necessary by killing them.'

'That's people just being human I suppose. But it is a fact that loads of people volunteer to try out new drugs. Perhaps there are those who would volunteer for our research. We could tell them that the likelihood of being harmed was low, but they might be in for a few shocks.'

'And extreme frights,' contributed Julie.

'Anyway, to be serious and moving on, you haven't told me how you're getting on with your family tree,' said Peter.

'Oh that. Well it's quite difficult, in fact impossible without more information. I'm going to have to visit my mum to get some leads, and I've decided to subscribe to an agency that offers to help you. There's one called Find My Past which sounds good. Enough for now. I think we've one or two bottles to open downstairs.'

CHAPTER THIRTY-EIGHT

———•———

'Of course I'm surprised, you knew I would be,' said Margaret, Julie's mother. 'You've never shown much interest before. Why, suddenly?'

Margaret's questions had been going on for several minutes.

'Oh, Mum. Of course I expected the Spanish Inquisition. But really …'

'Ha, I know that one. Nobody expected the Spanish Inquisition.'

They laughed. Margaret was not without a sense of humour and Julie was grateful she'd picked up on it while growing up, in spite of everything else going on in the family.

'But really,' she continued, 'I watched a few of those programmes where they research your family tree and I thought I'd like to try it.'

This was all true in fact. Julie had made sure of her preparation for this visit and could answer any questions about the programmes she had watched. These had been interestingly instructive, giving her tips on how to proceed with her own quest.

'Well, you know Granny and you knew Grandpa, but you know my mother's state from your visits to her. I don't suppose you'd get anything useful from her now. Still, you never know. Some people with dementia remember odd things. But you might get more information from the box. Sorry, I don't mean television; an actual box.'

'Box?' Julie felt a sudden optimism. A box. Anything could be in a box. A box could hold a multitude of secrets.

'It's in the spare room. Under the bed. I haven't looked at it for years and no one else in the family seems interested,' said Margaret.

'Perhaps someone soon will be. There's quite an interest in these TV programmes. I'd better make a claim on it, at least for a loan.'

'You can be the new guardian if you like but you'd better see what you're getting. You may change your mind.'

They went up to the spare bedroom and dragged the box from under the bed. Julie had imagined a tatty cardboard container. Instead it was a sturdy old wooden fruit crate with a worn label glued to an end showing a picture of a few red and rosy apples, apparently from New Zealand.

'Colonial fruit,' said Margaret wryly.

'Are there things like birth or marriage certificates in there?' asked Julie.

'There's all sorts. Receipts, photos, small items someone once wanted to keep. Hey, it's getting me interested now. Maybe I'll come over to go through it with you soon.'

'You'll be welcome. You can meet Peter.'

'Oh. What does Peter do then?'

'He's a teacher at my school. A science teacher.'

A silence fell as Julie and her mother recalled years of dispute caused by Julie's opposition to her father's use of science.

'Your father would have been pleased. Do you think they'd have got on?'

'I'm sure they would have.'

Margaret idly turned over some of the contents of the box. Another silence and Julie knew she was going to have to go into new territory. She reached out and took one of her mother's hands and waited until she had made eye contact.

'I know I've been contrite before but the older I get the deeper the sorrow gets. For the damage I did to us and the pain I caused you both. I became obsessed and frightened of the stuff they dealt with there. I kept reading more about those poisons and wished my father wasn't part of it.'

Margaret closed her eyes and remembered.

'You were right though. At least in some ways. He couldn't tell me anything about his work and I believed the lies they trotted out.'

They had been crouching over the box. Margaret, her hand still in Julie's, stood and pulled Julie to her feet, embracing her. Where once had been anger was now sadness.

'It was a dangerous sequence, starting in the First World War. One thing led to another. A bit like how the nuclear arms race developed. Your father and others believed the work was necessary to prevent war but I can tell you now, though you wouldn't have believed it at the time, that he understood your feelings and never stopped loving you.'

'I wish I'd gone about things in a different way,' said Julie.

Later that evening Peter received a text, which he guessed would need some explanation.

'Reconciled with Mum so staying over. She's making a cake for you so come for tea tomorrow and help me unload my treasure chest.'

He realised he would get nothing more until then so he focused on his 10K race next morning. Which turned out to be one of the usual disappointments. No matter how hard he trained he rarely won a race. Someone from somewhere would turn up to beat him. Be content, he thought. It's only running and you're always in the prizes.

By four o'clock the race was forgotten and he was anxious to hear what had been going on for Julie. By five he was just getting worried when a text arrived. 'Running late. Make it six.'

Running late reminded him of the race and he smiled at the apposite message.

CHAPTER THIRTY-NINE

———•———

Julie arrived in an upbeat but thoughtful mood with a hazelnut and honey cake and the box. Peter was surprised at the sheer weight of the thing, realising why she had called it a treasure chest.

'It's going to take ages to look through all this. I must see if there's anything like it in my family,' said Peter.

'I think family was much more important in the past,' said Julie. 'People went to the towns and cities so gradually lost the close contact, and as life changed there was less interest in past generations. Except now there might be a revival with TV programmes discovering ancestry. Also that programme A House Through Time, which is sort of related.'

'It's quite exciting looking at all this,' said Peter as Julie lifted the makeshift lid off the box. 'I hope you'll let me help with it.'

'Of course. I think it would be a great thing for us to share. Mm, get that hundred-year-old aroma.' Julie knelt to sniff all round the edges of the box's contents.

With a change of plans they decided to use the cake for dessert, so while Peter got together a salad and omelette, Julie went off to buy a couple of bottles of sweet wine. Half the cake had gone and the second bottle of wine begun before Peter broached the subject of Julie's mother and whatever had led to problems with their relationship.

'You really want to hear? It's not good. Especially my part. I was in a peace group, as were most of my friends, so it was a bit awkward that my dad worked at Porton Down. I'm sure you know all about that place. The best you can say is I became a real bore but the worst is that we weren't a happy family. I wasn't at all surprised to hear that those scientists hadn't been looking for a cure for the common cold at all, but had been testing Sarin on unsuspecting volunteers. All my dad would say is that everything had to be kept secret.'

'Did you ever get back on friendly terms with your dad?'

'No. That's the trouble. As soon as I left home for uni that was the end. And of course I regret it and I'm no wiser about what should be done. To me the world's weapons and means of delivery look like giant rat traps ready some day to be sprung. It's fearful. I used to sing songs around the house.'

Julie began singing a slow lilting song. 'Your mammy and pappy, they'll scrape and they'll save, build you a coffin and dig you a grave, hush-a-bye little one, why do you weep? We've got a toy that will put you to sleep. Sang the crow on the cradle.

'I may have mixed a few lines but you get the idea. A lot of young people are deciding not to bring children into the world and that's such a shame. I used to think I'd be able to tell my children, "well at least I tried", but that doesn't seem to matter any more does it?'

Peter was at a loss for words. With her memories and the wine, Julie was crying quietly. He crouched next to her chair and held her for several minutes. She raked a tissue from her sleeve and blew her nose noisily, then met Peter's eyes and smiled.

'I'm not going to apologise. It's all been a bit superficial really, you and me. We chat and laugh and have great sex but we've steered away from anything deeper, either consciously or not.'

'Consciously I think,' said Peter. 'We don't want to find there are huge differences in our morals or politics. I might be a secret member of the British National Party and you might go fox hunting on those days I'm not around. So far we've just kept on the safe side and assumed our views were liberal and humanist enough.'

Julie didn't answer at first but walked unsteadily to the box and began turning over the topmost papers.

'It's strange in a way. Probably all the people mentioned or documented here are dead. What would they have thought of us? We've been pretty casual, whereas they would have been far more formal. Marriage and children would have been the important matters. Look, Peter, this weekend's been a bit much and this wine is going to give me a headache so can you go home tonight?'

'That's fine. Too much sweet stuff. What were we thinking of? I'm pretty tired anyway.'

'Oh, Peter. You had a race and I haven't asked how it went. I'm sorry.'

'I was trying to avoid it. Fifth if you must know. I won a torch.'

Julie laughed. 'So you'll find your way home OK then.'

When Peter had gone, Julie sat and gazed at her box, lost in thought.

CHAPTER FORTY

S everal weeks after Julie had spoken to Paul to discover if he remembered anything unusual during the visit to the air crash site, he sought her out one lunchtime with news that he'd carried out some research on his great grandfather.

'It turns out he was a fairly serious cricketer. Played for Berkshire in the Minor Counties. And, guess what – he was a batsman! Remember linseed oil?'

Julie was immediately delighted.

'That's fascinating, Paul. Or might be. We have to keep a level head about these things.'

'Maybe, but it's beginning to sound a bit like some sort of ghost story, isn't it?'

'Maybe. Anyway, thanks for finding that out.'

'Something else,' Paul went on. 'I was thinking about the memories drifting in fields thing. If people could somehow pick up on them, wouldn't young children be likely recipients? You know, before their minds got too involved with their own world?'

'That's good thinking. It might explain why our, what shall we call them, visions, faded.'

Pressure of work for Peter and Julie eased off as the summer term drew to a close. Amid the general relaxation the exam-takers evaporated. The Science Group went on meeting until the penultimate week of term. Selwood's visit had raised interest in the club and, with the older sixth formers leaving, Peter was preparing for the following year's sessions. He was hoping the visit could be repeated for the benefit of new members but knew it was a lot to ask of someone so busy. Still, no harm in trying and Peter compiled a list of experiments both proposed and carried out to attract the scientist.

They had agreed to spend at least half the summer break apart. Julie had been invited by an old friend to share a cottage in the south of

France and Peter had arranged to go camping in Scotland with his housemate. The first week of the school break for Julie was devoted to clearing the debris of the past year and laying down some ideas for the next. Since the following three weeks were to be spent in France, she had little time to start on the contents of the family box. Any session she did start was soon arrested by a particular letter or document and the real task of tracing her ancestry was totally neglected.

Julie loved being immersed in one of the languages she taught and always had more to learn. On this trip she picked up many words and phrases concerning the weather, which mainly consisted of gales and heavy rain causing flooding and landslides.

Returning to Britain she was aggrieved to hear of the weeks of dry hot weather that had blessed Peter and Brian's camping trip and to see their pronounced suntans.

'Wasn't it meant to be the other way round?' was her rueful comment.

'Wait until you hear about all the wildlife we saw,' said Peter mischievously.

'Yes, and I'll tell you all about Gallic rain,' replied Julie.

Peter came round on the second evening with the box now the focus of their attention. Peter was interested to see how their relationship had fared after the break. In fact, as he hoped, it was as if they'd never been apart. One day soon, he promised himself, he would broach the subject of living together, since this idea had never been even hinted at. He knew Julie well enough now to recognise the importance of independence, so was quite prepared for her to reject the possibility of cohabitation. Importantly, he must try to avoid conflict over the lake disaster.

They decided to sift through the contents of the box quickly to separate all items that might help with ancestry research and resist the temptation to meander through all the rest, however interesting looking. There was plenty of material to help in the form of birth, death and marriage certificates and over the next few evenings they had established a good deal of a family tree. It would be easier, they realised, if people hadn't had so many children in the past. With the help of the Find My Past agency they had reached back to the mid-nineteenth century, which was when possible relatives would have lived. There were many names to investigate, but many of these people would have had nothing to do with Julie's past family.

But within ten minutes of starting their fourth daily sift, Julie's life changed. She looked at the seemingly innocuous marriage certificate and held her breath, then gave a surprised exclamation. Peter looked up from his own reading. Julie's face was drained of colour and, wordless, she pointed to the aged, creased document. Peter read of the marriage between Dafydd Morgan and Tillie Hopkins. This meant nothing to him but Julie suddenly rushed to her laptop, though she hardly needed to. Several names had made an impression when she had first compiled a list of lake disaster victims and Dafydd, likely a Welshman, had not been forgotten. Looking then at the complicated maze they had constructed of past family, they found her. Married name Tillie Morgan. The percentage probability that Tillie was a distant ancestor of Julie's was estimated by Find My Past to be in the nineties. To Julie, her link to the lake was now fact.

She disappeared and returned with a bottle of Tequila. She poured two glasses, her hands trembling with excitement.

'Better not drink too much of that,' said Peter.

'Oh, why not?' said Julie excitedly. 'Let's at least get squiffy. We might be on the brink of something wonderful.'

Julie had never doubted that a memory of the lake event had somehow been bequeathed to her directly. But surely, Peter had always reasoned, such a disaster in a family's past would resonate, however faintly, down the generations. It wouldn't take much more than a mention as Julie was growing up for a seed to be sown, waiting for the very prompt which Paul had provided at the Science Group. Previously, Julie had shown annoyance with him when he'd said something that she saw as sceptical. Scientists had to be critical, but if what Julie believed was in fact true, then an extraordinary event had occurred. He resolved, for the time being, to put aside any doubts. He joined Julie in a celebratory drink. Even if her story turned out to be true, the likelihood of anyone else believing it was very low. It would, perhaps, just seem another apocryphal tale.

CHAPTER FORTY-ONE

F or Julie it was certainty. The line from the distant Tillie ran through the many generations to herself and the memory derived from the lake disaster was real and meaningful, though what the meaning was she had no idea. There was no established science that could explain or accept it, but that mattered not a bit to Julie, who felt she was just at the beginning of a mysterious journey and was loving it. Peter had eventually stated his, to Julie, dreary doubts, but she hardly minded, feeling as she did the glow of success. She did agree to share her discovery with her mother and to ask whether there had ever been to her knowledge any talk of Regent's Park or people called Dafydd or Tillie.

Julie dearly wanted to tear into the family box so that she could flesh out the tree with all the material they had deliberately ignored. But with the school break soon coming to an end and much to do before the autumn term her good sense, and Peter's, toned down her desire. They rationed themselves to forty minutes a session, this being the length of periods at school. They knew through the first sorting that someone had stratified the contents, so the oldest material, where they had come across Tillie and Dafydd, was near the bottom. There were several fragments of diaries that could be used to cross reference family members but it wasn't until they arrived at the First World War that a really full diary appeared and this was written in the tiniest handwriting so that reading it took several sessions. The diarist had been a hospital nurse in Birmingham and had been much involved with military casualties. One bold soldier had clearly captured her heart and, following his discharge from the hospital, they began a courtship that lasted through his convalescence. They were both fearful that he would be returning to the front, but that part of their story had a happy ending with the end of the war. They fitted nicely into the family tree. For the first time Julie understood some of the emotions felt by people on the past relatives programmes. A mixture of pride and sadness.

The autumn term began and life resumed a regular pattern. Julie started rehearsing new pieces with the school orchestra and Peter resumed his extra-curricular Science Group. During the last few days of the holiday Peter had suggested that they consider living together. Julie showed no surprise so had obviously been considering the issue, but neither of them could sort out the pros and cons so shelved it for the time being. Julie was feeling herself safe from undue compulsions, which could, with luck, be a lasting state of mind.

But lying in wait for more than a hundred and forty years, like a snare, was a diary. The diary was enclosed in a package that hadn't been looked at during their first search. With it was a marriage certificate registering the marriage of Tillie Morgan to George Yeoman. Tillie had married twice! Julie, in a state of high excitement, carefully turned the pages of the diary. The contents of the package were fragile. Julie realised that she should probably adopt the precautions that museums take by wearing delicate cotton gloves. Peter agreed. The papers here were too valuable, to them at least, to risk further deterioration. There were no gloves in Julie's house and, since they had begun late it was well into the evening, so Julie reluctantly placed the bundle back in the box.

CHAPTER FORTY-TWO

'I've really been looking forward to this.'

Julie was eager to start and had taken out the diary as soon as they met for their evening search.

They began going through the diary sentence by sentence. The first entry started with a complete surprise.

'Wow, she actually heard Charles Dickens!' exclaimed Julie.

Moving on through the diary, they learned of the author's changes of circumstances and began to get a picture of the times she lived in and the people in her life. As she became familiar with the characters, Julie had to remind herself that these had been real people, some of whom were her distant relatives. By the time they reached the lake tragedy both Peter and Julie were involved enough to be moved by the account and the shattering effect on all their lives. Following Dafydd's death, the day-to-day references to Tillie and her children were fewer as they had moved away from the Primrose Hill district that had been their home following Tillie's marriage to Dafydd. The close friendship continued, however, and any events in Tillie's life were noted and visits were common. As social history alone the whole journal was valuable and fascinating. They pieced together as best they could the lives of the characters they were most interested in. There were many references to fires and accidents that the writer's husband had attended, one of which Julie managed to trace in the newspaper archive. She was hoping that amongst the dregs of the box there would be information to fill gaps, especially the name and details of the writer. They looked through the papers they had examined previously to see if there was a marriage certificate, but that document had either been lost or had gone elsewhere.

Several months before the journal ended, the writer became pregnant. This was clearly a great joy to her but thereafter the entries became shorter, with days missing. Then they stopped.

'So what do we know so far?' asked Peter.

'Well, we know she was an important friend of Tillie, which is the thing that matters to me most. We know she'd been a domestic servant and seems to have worked for Tillie as such. Then she changed to working in the shop run by the Yeomans. She marries George Yeoman, but we know that George Yeoman marries Tillie years later. Whatever happened to bring that about we don't know.'

'You can see that the four of them were close friends. The diarist, George Yeoman, Dafydd and Tillie. But I'm only related to Dafydd and Tillie. I'm sure my dream experiences concerned only them.'

Julie went over to her armchair and relaxed back into it. The diary had unlocked all the secrets it was going to and the London of the 1860s was beginning to feel as real as her life in modern Gloucester. She wished the woman who had written the diary had been at the lake on the day of the accident. A first-hand account by someone they knew something about would be much better than a newspaper report. They had no information on how George had rescued Lilian.

'All that stuff about Primrose Hill,' sighed Julie. 'I must go there. I want to be where all this happened to those people.'

'We can have another trip there,' said Peter hopefully.

There was a silence while Julie considered this.

'I hope you won't mind but I'd like to be alone there. I'd be better at visualising if I'm not distracted.'

Peter did mind in fact. He also would like to contemplate the district they had been reading about but he had never imposed his company on Julie and didn't intend to start now. They were both occupied after school for the next few days, so it wasn't until the following Monday that they were able to resume the last stages of the box research. Within ten minutes they made a thrilling discovery. Tillie's own handwriting.

'My dearest friend, Jean Yeoman, died yesterday with blood poisoning. Her baby boy is thriving and my parents and I have undertaken his welfare for the time being with George's consent. We have found a wet nurse for him. We have shared so much and we were hoping to share more as our children grew. Jean came to us distressed and became family. Though I returned to the farm a widow, not a week went by without our spending some time together. I treasure the memories.'

The sheet of paper on which this was written had been folded in half and held together with a fragment of sealing wax that had long ago failed. On what would have been the outside was written 'By Hand'.

'It's like it was written for us,' whispered Julie.

They both stared at the scrap of paper.

'So Jean is the diarist. I wish George or another of the Yeomans had also kept a diary. Then we could have found out more about her. We don't even know her maiden name,' Julie continued.

'Maybe a census would give us information,' suggested Peter.

'Maybe. But it's Tillie and her descendants that interest me. It's frustrating to think about all those possible leads from the family tree that we haven't followed up. We could pass distant relatives of mine any day in the street. I would bet they know nothing about the lake, like me before. Isn't it strange how things fade?'

CHAPTER FORTY-THREE

———◆———

Julie booked two nights in a small hotel in Belsize Park for the last few days of half-term week. Her pilgrimage, as she thought of it, might not need that length of time but she could look around the rest of London as well. After dinner she sat in her room watching the light fade. The trees in the street were giving up their greenery, which brought to her mind their last find in the family box; one that had actually made her cry. The small, tattered remains of Tillie's pressed flowers, amongst them tiny fragments of the daffodil that Dafydd had brought back from his first trip as a passenger train driver. Only part of Tillie's note giving the specimen's provenance was legible, but there was enough to identify the item. There was no real reason to preserve the remnants of Tillie's collection, but neither Peter nor Julie felt like binning them.

Julie had re-read what they now knew as Jean's diary and had gathered as much data as possible about connections to the characters mentioned during the period 1865 to 1867. So, next morning, with A-to-Z map book in hand, she set off eagerly on her mission to bring to life in her own mind those long-lost lives. The Yeomans had run their fruit and vegetable shop in Regent's Park Road and this was her first call. The weather was perfect; one of those early autumn days you wish would be followed by an exact copy, then another, possibly forever. Julie was comfortable in a light top and slacks but carried a jacket in case her day ran into the evening.

Her walk took her alongside Primrose Hill with a descent directly to Regent's Park Road. She had read a little of the history of the hill itself. Apparently there had been a massive naval gun mounted at the top during the Second World War on anti-aircraft duties. Whether or not it hit anything was unknown but many local people lost sleep when it was firing. A V2 rocket had landed on the lower slope, causing no harm to property or higher life forms. Had there ever been primroses? Allotments had covered the area during the 'dig for victory' campaign.

She began a slow walk along Regent's Park Road. This is gentrification gone mad, as they say, was her thought. Bistros and small restaurants seemed to line the street punctuated by galleries and boutiques. Just as expected, she saw that you have to be pretty wealthy to live round here. Julie had been making copies of all the old photographs she could find in the last few weeks. This collection she now took out and began selecting those that matched what she could see. The images didn't go back to Tillie's day of course but if you looked above the posh street-level frontages not much had changed in the last hundred years.

The thing was, where had her characters lived? She had studied Jean's writing and looked at old maps so had some idea of where Yeoman's greengrocery had traded. The road was only half built in the early 1860s, so the choice was narrowed considerably. It was only a short distance to her favoured location on the opposite side. She was certain at once. The premises now housed an upmarket children's clothes shop and three down from that a bookshop traded where Tillie must have lived. Julie stood and gazed and without difficulty conjured up the people she felt she now knew. There was Tillie, hand in hand with Lilian, hurrying from her house to the shop. There was big dependable George Yeoman arranging carrots and swedes in a pavement display as he contemplated proposing to Jean, who she could see inside serving a customer. And here came tough jovial Dafydd home from shovelling coal into the firebox of an engine.

'Are you all right, dear?'

Julie jumped and tried to focus on the twenty-first century. She turned and met the anxious eyes of a slightly built middle-aged woman, who for a second she thought might be Jean Yeoman come to haunt her.

'Only you were standing there so long I wondered if you were taken with something.'

Jean laughed, glad to be herself again.

'No, no. I'm sorry to worry you. Truthfully I was back in the 1860s.'

'Oh?'

Julie wondered if the stranger would really be interested in the story. She would soon be able to decide and in fact she would quite like to share with someone who actually lived locally, assuming this woman did.

'I'm descended from a woman who lived round here in 1867. Probably just over there.' Julie pointed to the building she thought she'd identified.

'That's amazing. How do you know? Did you pay for one of these agencies that trace ancestors?'

'That's right. Do you live locally?'

'Camden Town. Rent's a bit cheaper. I work part time in a fashion shop along the road here. I'm not on 'til this afternoon so I've plenty of time for a coffee. Would you like to join me? I'd love to hear about this ancestor of yours.'

The woman, who introduced herself as Pamela, guided Julie to her usual cafe and sat down expectantly. Julie was glad to find someone so receptive. She was intrigued to discover how a complete stranger would react to her story, although it was tricky to know where to begin. So she started with the Science Group and described Paul's dream experience, which led to her own recollection. Pamela seemed fascinated and it seemed safe to go on to how she came across the lake disaster.

'From there it seemed sensible to find out if some sort of family relationship existed. You see, Paul wondered if his vision was connected to his great grandfather who was killed during the Second World War in a mid-air collision.'

'So you really think,' said Pamela slowly, 'that your dream experience came down to you through all that time from this ancestor of yours.'

Julie felt she had to be cautious. 'I think it's possible, that's all.'

'And you're here to what, somehow close the circle?'

This suggestion startled Julie, as did Pamela's quick perspicacity.

'Why do you say that? I'm sorry; that's a bit abrupt of me, but it's just that I've had a feeling for some time that there's something I have to do and you seem to have touched on that immediately.'

'Well, it's just that I could see you were very involved. Perhaps more than just out of curiosity.'

Julie had thought of this trip and her previous visit with Peter as pilgrimages but perhaps, after all, there was something asked of her. The vague fantasy that had occasionally touched her over the past two months suddenly came into focus. Pamela was proving to be a catalyst to her thinking.

'You know you may be right. It's possible that my destiny lies out there someday on the ice. Sounds a bit melodramatic I know.'

Pamela felt a tingle, a mix of excitement and dread. Who was this strange woman who, in a few minutes, was stirring her emotions more deeply than had many people she'd known for years?

'You mean you'll go out on the lake when it's frozen?' she asked in wonder.

'It could be what I'm called on to do,' said Julie.

'I'm not sure they let people do that.'

'Then I'll go at night.' There was a pause. 'Did I say that?'

'You did and I hope you didn't mean it. I'm getting frightened for you,' said Pamela.

'Don't worry. After the 1867 disaster they drained the lake and made it much shallower, so even in the worst case I'll be safe.'

Pamela looked doubtful. 'Doesn't matter how shallow it is, it'll still be bloody cold.'

'Yes,' Julie pondered. 'Perhaps I should wear a wet suit or something. I don't have one. I prefer swimming when I can feel the water.'

'Maybe, but not in a lake in the middle of winter,' said Pamela. 'Unless you were hoping for ice at a more temperate time of year,' she joked. 'Anyway, won't you have some sort of back-up? Someone to help you?'

'I have this feeling I have to be alone if it happens.'

'Look, I have to do some shopping before my shift, but can I give you my number? I'm very interested now so would like you to call me if I can help in any way? I'd like to hear more of those people who worked and lived in this street.'

Pamela departed, leaving Julie to mull over their conversation. The light-hearted curiosity she'd woken to had quite suddenly been given a purpose. As to what lay behind it, she could only hope that clarity would come with time.

CHAPTER FORTY-FOUR

Julie continued her journey but discovered that her feelings had undergone a sea change since setting out that morning. There was now a purpose to this visit and all the knowledge she had gained recently, but that purpose lay in an unseen world. Julie called to mind Halloween, which was quite close. The veil between the living and the spiritual realm was supposed to be thinnest on that day. She had never particularly gone along with the idea of ghosts and poltergeists but, having read Selwood's book and been involved in the Science Group, she could accept that there existed a domain seemingly, for the present, hidden from conventional science. A domain in which all of us and all life for that matter had a place. A place possibly of mind and imagination that we both ignore and take for granted. Although she didn't expect to understand her link with Tillie she now knew that she could be driven to stand, alone and at night, at the centre of the frozen lake. That it made no rational sense was obvious to her, but there had always been, linked to her dream, a feeling of something unaccomplished – a dislocation of some kind. The crazy, hazardous act she planned would perhaps be a conclusion. Although she had made light of it with Pamela, she realised the danger involved. She could only think that the risk was a necessary factor.

She followed the route that Jean and George had taken, one evening in the past, walking down to the canal. At that stage Jean was wondering if George was intending to court her. How things change yet at heart remain the same. To Julie these were real people to the extent that she now longed to meet them. They would discuss all sorts of things. How amazed they would be at what she could tell them. Electricity, huge jet aircraft, atomic bombs. Yet they had been in at the genesis of these things and might in fact be more interested in changes to domestic life – fridges and washing machines. Perhaps they wouldn't be shocked. These were the streets they had walked and through which

George had pulled his cart of vegetables on the delivery round. As she walked she felt she could easily push aside the curtains of time and make an entrance, as in a play, onto the stage of the nineteenth century.

The streets here had always been quiet, she supposed, since there were no through routes. The peacefulness helped her imaginings and she was intrigued by the changes, or sometimes lack of changes, when comparing present reality with her old photos. She reached the school that had been built on the field Jean and George had visited on their walk. Here they must have paused to watch the working horses wandering. Perhaps had fed them an apple or two. The large red-brick building was empty today; it must be half-term here too. The multi-paned windows looked back benignly, returning Julie's gaze. So much history locked behind them. Perhaps descendants of Tillie had attended this school. Did they ever dream of the lake and sorrow?

The next stop was Primrose Hill itself. Julie hoped to find the oak tree that had been planted on the day George proposed to Jean, given that oak trees had such long lives. The area seemed bigger than she expected and after wandering for a while without success she spotted a park attendant and explained her quest. Fortunately he knew something of the hill's history.

'Well, the original tree died. Oaks don't do very well on Primrose Hill, nor do primroses actually. I'm told they planted a replacement for the 1864 one in 1964 complete with a plaque, but because the plaque was stolen it was decided not to waste any more money on them. There are still a few oaks but no one knows which is the commemorative one.'

This minor disappointment was forgotten as she approached the lake. She stopped and gazed out across the water and knew in a flash why it was that she'd experienced two seemingly irrelevant recollections last time she'd stood here. Those memories both had strong associations with something not completed. This time that feeling was here directly. It was powerful and she quickly turned her back and walked away, crossing the bridges spanning one of the lake's backwaters. She found a bench near the children's boating pond. The activities of the children provided a distraction, allowing her emotions to settle. As she became calmer she began to anticipate Peter's reactions to her plan. She had to be ready whatever he said and if he suggested that all this was solely in her mind, brain, whatever, then she would point out that there were some pretty strange twists in the laws of chance during her recent months. She now felt more convinced that she was a part of something real. Being a musician she sought for a musical metaphor that might describe her present life. Perhaps Ravel and his Bolero with its relentless heartbeat, swaying movement, akin to her moods, and final wild crescendo.

Well, nothing could happen until winter and even then there had to be a cold spell long enough, and winters were less cold these days. What was needed was high pressure over northern Europe, settled conditions over Britain with long clear frosty nights. She needed to be prepared. The park would be closed at night. She walked over to the iron railings that marked the boundary. The notebook from her bag was a good unit of measurement and the dimensions of the railings were transferred onto a sketch. It obviously wouldn't be possible to carry any sort of ladder around, so something from rope would have to be contrived. Nobody bothered her while she was measuring and, had they done so, she had her story ready. She was an artist preparing for a series of watercolours. No, of course she wasn't planning to break into the park in the middle of the night in the middle of the winter. Whoever heard of such a thing! After all, the railings were too high; all of eight notebooks.

There was one more place to be visited and that was the site of the old fruit and vegetable market at Covent Garden. There were many mentions of the market in Jean's diary, though infuriatingly no actual address for the Yeoman family home. The old buildings themselves were not massive but had an industrial poignancy, especially when Julie took out the copies of photographs taken when the market was thriving. These images showed people whose lives were of hard constant labour. The Yeomans would have been amazed at the high-class retail businesses that now occupied their old haunts.

Julie felt she had absorbed all she could concerning her friends from the nineteenth century, for so she now regarded them. In her mind a countdown had begun to a decisive act which would resolve the many questions which had arisen for herself and Peter. She hoped. She decided to spend the rest of the day near the Thames which she had loved in the past. A short walk to and along the Embankment brought her to Cleopatra's Needle which had always captivated her imagination. From many centuries of hot desert lands, to stand forever amid the climatic vicissitudes of London, was a strange destiny. Julie imagined its looming presence in the lonely yellow London smogs she had heard about.

Lunchtime was well past and Julie was hungry and wishing she still smoked. After tearing herself away from the monolith she continued to walk along the river and discovered one of the vessels offering trips was about to leave. There was no way of resisting this; her stomach would have to wait and make do with a couple of peppermints.

As soon as the launch had left the jetty Julie was glad she'd taken this opportunity. The vessel surged against the ebbing tide, rocking rhythmically with the waves the Thames conjured up from somewhere. Even sitting in a seat on a passenger launch there was a sense of freedom out on the wide expanses of the river. The eternal breezes and smells, the dynamic rushes and echoes under the great arches of the bridges were there for anyone and Julie felt a quiet, detached joy.

CHAPTER FORTY-FIVE

———•———

There was nothing to be gained by staying longer. Julie could now picture the buildings and streets in which her friends had lived. She would re-read Jean's diary and be able to bring them all to life in her imagination. She was feeling towards them something unexpected, strange. She realised, shocked, that it was love. Leaving the hotel early on her second morning, she travelled by tube to Paddington Station, from which she would depart on her homeward journey. Before that, however, it was also the place where she would call on her imagination to bring to life two important people. Jean had related in her diary that Dafydd had worked out of Paddington firstly as a fireman and later as a driver. She had also relayed from Tillie the story of her first meeting with Dafydd, how she had been travelling home from a visit to an aunt when a man jumped down from the footplate of a locomotive and captivated her. Dafydd must have possessed an extraordinary charm to get away with such an approach without being repulsed.

It was with this image in mind that Julie walked out under the great echoing roof of Paddington Station. Of course she had no idea where the meeting had taken place so explored several platforms until she found a likely location. A convenient bench provided a place to recreate the genesis of Tillie and Dafydd's romance. Here comes Tillie carrying her luggage obtained from her aunt, and who is this sweaty, powerful-looking man stepping down from his engine and pacing rapidly towards her? Tillie looks alarmed. Dafydd's body language is confident but reassuring. He smiles broadly and speaks. Tillie visibly relaxes and looks away, but she is smiling.

Julie replayed the scene with variations several times, but how the two had been feeling she couldn't guess. Wonderful though that it led to them marrying.

Sweeping out of London in a train that would have amazed Dafydd, Julie tried to restore order to her mind. Her main focus was on the wild adventurous act she planned, that probably only she would believe had any purpose. But her visit had once more brought to mind the contrast between her relationship with Peter and that of Tillie and her husband. Although she and Peter had discussed living together they had shelved the idea for now. Marriage had never entered the conversation, let alone the possibility of children. Compared to their Victorian counterparts the relationship had developed in a very informal way. What struck her as she considered it was the comfortableness she felt with Peter. She herself had initiated the friendship and had since guided it to suit her own needs, enjoying the sex, keeping her independence and appreciating his constant attention. She doubted she matched Peter's feelings, yet if asked would say, yes, of course I love him. But was there passion? And was this passion that she was beginning to feel about her mission?

Julie wondered how to present her plan to Peter; or would she present it at all? Perhaps she would keep it to herself until the time came to execute it. That would avoid the objections she expected, but could she do it, and would a secret of this magnitude change their relationship? She needed time to decide so sent a text message to Peter to say she wanted the evening alone, then relaxed to enjoy the rest of the journey, especially the minute spent looking up at the houses piled seemingly one on top of another that was the precipitous village of Chalford Hill. She was home.

CHAPTER FORTY-SIX

The following day, the last weekday of the half term, Peter rang to say he would come round for the afternoon if that was convenient. Julie agreed, despite not knowing yet how or whether to share her intentions. She realised she needed some continuing reassurance so their prolonged hug in the hallway was welcome, as was Peter's enthusiasm to hear about her London journey. Was this just general interest or was he thinking in scientific terms? She cautiously began by describing the river trip then, in reverse, her musings on Cleopatra's Needle and then back further to Covent Garden.

Since Peter was giving good attention, she went back to the beginning in Regent's Park Road, describing how the characters from Jean's diary became almost tangible and her growing affection for them. This then was the parting of the ways. If she didn't confide now it was going to be difficult later on and out of context. She described how Pamela had interrupted her reverie with the best of intentions and how they had then shared morning coffee.

'Pamela was fascinated by my story and, this is the important bit, Peter, suggested that I could close the circle. Exactly what circle remains a mystery, but from the moment she said that I knew I had to one day go out on the frozen lake. My destiny. I know that sounds melodramatic but I don't have any doubts about it. And before you say it, I realise that the whole thing could be in my own mind. But that doesn't matter. Something will happen out there, though I've no idea what. Something will be resolved for me that needs to be. It could be just guilt. A penance.'

Peter realised that his reaction to what seemed to be an irrevocable decision was going to be important. If this was chess, Julie had put him in check by including the possibility that everything in the last few months had been imaginary, but that notwithstanding, real enough to put her dangerous plan into action. But if it was all based on actual memory echoes from the past then she had a good basis for her expectation. After all, she claimed that the feelings of sadness and loss she experienced in her early dream had never gone away but had stayed dormant through her life, to be awakened by hearing of Paul's experience. But then, reasoned Peter, maybe everyone is touched by distant echoes without ever realising. Julie could have lived the rest of her life without ever knowing of the disaster in her family past. Would never have known Tillie and the rest. If there was something needing resolution it would never happen. Would it matter? Julie was waiting for a response.

'Will I be a part of this venture? I would feel happier if I could be on hand in case you are in danger.'

'I know you would and I knew you would ask. Of course I would feel safer if you were to be around. But the element of risk is integral and I just know that the event wouldn't occur if I had a safety net. We have to remember that Tillie saw her husband drown without being able to help in any way. I wish Jean had described how George rescued Lilian. Did he have to choose between Lilian and Dafydd? We would have a clearer idea of what happened if Jean had been with them. There are things we might never know unless my event, as I call it, gives me a clue.'

Peter was clearly unhappy to be discounted as a support.

'Where does this put our relationship now?' he said.

'In one way it will put some stress on it and I'll tell you why. You see, after today I don't want to discuss my plan or theories or evidence. Nothing at all, and it will be difficult for both of us, especially when the weather gets cold. The best support you can be is to agree never to mention the issue until it's over. Can you do that?'

'I suppose if they could keep D-Day plans secret I can keep quiet about this. It'll be just you and me in on it then. Oh, and there's that Pamela.'

Julie looked thoughtful. 'Yes, she'll have to be eliminated of course.'

Peter took up the joke.

'How shall we do it?'

'I know where she has morning coffee. It'll have to be poison.'

'Seriously though, I haven't known you to be so, well, definite, or even dominant before,' said Peter.

'Mmm, well, I haven't wanted to tell you before ...'

Peter smiled.

'No, this is on the level. Oh God, what with teaching, your running, my fantasies, there's a lot we don't know about each other's past. As I said, I haven't wanted to tell you before for various reasons. One, I was ashamed, and for another I wanted to be different, or at least not end up how I did before.'

Peter frowned. What on earth was coming next?

Julie began massaging her left-hand fingers that were so agile on the neck of the violin, something Peter had noticed before when she was concentrating. She began hesitantly.

'You remember I told you my last serious relationship became closed in and failed. What I led you to assume by omission was that my partner had dominated me. In fact that was not the case. I was the oppressor. Well, that's the wrong word really. It was to do with our respective personalities. Something that became more and more difficult and in the end intolerable to me.'

'But you told me he was one of these super strong weightlifting types. Difficult to see him as pushed around in any way.'

'Well, as they say, appearances are deceptive. Oh I didn't try to beat him up or anything, though I felt frustrated enough at times. He was just so weak in all other ways; as if he wanted to be directed or pushed or bullied even. Of course, it wasn't noticeable at first. Or maybe I found it too easy to be the boss. But pretty soon I was finding that I had to take the lead in everything. Make all the decisions. At the same time he became more possessive. It got to be claustrophobic. I wonder if he found anyone suited to the role. Or maybe he changed.'

'So you saw weedy-looking me and guessed I would be strong in other ways,' said Peter ruefully.

'No, I just thought you were cute,' laughed Julie.

Peter went home for the night, attempting to piece together his thoughts. He had become used to Julie springing surprises but this revelation about her past was a shock to his complacent view of her and their relationship. By being, as he thought, sensitive and not asking any questions, he had allowed her to mislead him even by omission, as she had said. He just had to accept that it was done with good intentions.

Since neither of them had preparatory work for school they had arranged to spend time together over the weekend. Then they'd be back to work. The last half term of the year had taken them into winter and the possible chance for Julie to carry out her plan. Until then there would be a constant backdrop to their lives. Dafydd, Tillie, Lilian and Owen, Jean and George, whether real or imagined, would be waiting.

CHAPTER FORTY-SEVEN

The school term rolled on, the leaves fell and the days grew short. Julie found that she now lived on two levels. Her teaching, as always, took the greater part of her time. Students who had been in her classes before noticed small changes. There were fewer of the by-plays she had always used and her usual vivacity was muted. What was not visible to anyone else was the empty stage Julie saw, set for a drama that had been scripted for her. She valued the times when life seemed almost normal: orchestra rehearsals for the Christmas concert, intense physical effort at the gym she had recently joined. She wondered what would happen if she dropped the whole thing, forgot the lake, forgot Tillie and the disaster. Impossible to live with was the conclusion. The scientific aspect of her experience – what many would term pseudo-science – interested her intensely. As a beginning of a research project that she fully intended to pursue she asked several people if they remembered any repetitive dreams from infancy. Considering the tiny sample the result was encouraging. A woman when asked gave an animated description of a tsunami. Julie was careful to ask whether it could have been an ordinary memory, say of a film or even a photo image. These were going to be difficult to eliminate in future investigations, but if there was any substance to the theory of inherited memory then you would have to consider the possibility that many, if not all, lives were affected, perhaps mainly unawares.

Their intimacy was comforting to both Peter and Julie in different ways. Julie could dismiss thoughts of the future. Although that was not possible for Peter, there was reassurance every time they slept together. Julie found it endearing that since the revelation of her past character Peter was making it a point to be more forceful in discussions and decision making. She assured him that there was no similarity in the relationships. Or not much, she sometimes added with tongue in cheek.

Just as Julie speculated about the effects of changing her plan, Peter also wondered if that was possible and came to the same conclusion. The die was cast. There were occasions when their eyes met in silence and a profound awareness of unspoken thoughts reminded them that this period was a hiatus in their separate and combined lives.

CHAPTER FORTY-EIGHT

Term ended with no sign of real winter weather. During Christmas Julie and Peter travelled north, Julie meeting Peter's father for the first time, along with his sister and several cousins. She was disconcerted to discover that the family members she met had all voted to leave the European Union, in contrast to the views she knew Peter held. He had not been at all surprised and joked on the way home that he'd always been the odd one out.

The spring term began. Exams were on the horizon for many of the students. There was new music for the orchestra and Peter had begun coaching sessions for promising runners. Julie made hopeful preparations for her mission and watched weather forecasts every day. Peter also monitored them but his hopes were for a continued mild winter. He would, if it were possible, admit to anyone that he feared for Julie's safety. Unfortunately, there was no one he could confide in under his girlfriend's strict censorship.

In mid-February Peter's fears gained ground. High pressure was building in northern Europe. A sudden change in Britain's weather brought a dry cold that quickly intensified. He noticed with a sinking heart how Julie had become animated, but with great self-control restrained from broaching the subject of her excitement. Talk about the elephant in the room, he thought, as the couple tried to keep ordinary conversation going. He rather saw it though, as a seal. Sliding across ice and plunging into freezing water.

Julie saw the opportunity coming. She began filling the bird bath every evening and each morning her hopes grew with the depth of ice. She was having difficulty keeping her relationship with Peter on an even keel. Getting to sleep was also a problem, though less so when she was in bed with Peter. As a new week started she would have preferred them not to meet at all, but that would be tantamount to announcing her departure. She could feel Peter's frustration and felt sorry that he wasn't able to share in what was to be, she hoped, a major event in her life. As a second freezing week progressed the weather became a major news item. Julie booked a ticket to London for Thursday evening. What to do about Peter? She felt enormous appreciation for the patience he had shown. It would be impossible just to go without a way of thanking him. She decided to leave a letter. If she avoided him all day he would know she had left and would undoubtedly call at her house.

Thursday came with bitterly cold winds seeded by hard snow particles. Julie had gathered her equipment in the hallway to be collected before catching the train. She looked back at it before closing the door and was satisfied she could not have improved on her preparations. The day passed slowly. She knew how to avoid Peter just as in normal times she knew how to snatch an odd minute with him. She had turned off her phone, an action which alone would alert him. To be absolutely certain she had enlisted the help of Anne, the orchestra leader, who had agreed to catch Peter at the end of the day, letting him know of her departure. Anne was extremely curious. Where was she going on such a night and why? There was no longer any point in secrecy. Anne was to tell Peter he had her, Julie's, permission to describe the mission and its history. She had booked a day's leave for the next day so, one way or another, anyone interested would soon know all about it.

Peter's students noticed the pauses as the day passed. Peter would uncharacteristically lose the thread for moments as he struggled to avoid thinking about Julie. The hours passed as slowly for him as they did for Julie and his apprehension grew when he was caught by Anne as he hurried from the school. She confirmed what he had feared, that Julie was travelling to London that evening. Anne was, of course, intensely curious and assured Peter that she had been granted access to the secret, but there was no way that Peter was going to waste even a minute to explain. He had previously decided on a course of action in this situation and there was no time to lose. Merely saying that it was a long story, he dashed away, leaving Anne as mystified as ever.

Julie's house was in darkness. He was too late. On the hall floor was an unsealed envelope from which, with trembling hands, he drew her letter.

'My dearest Peter,

The time has come and I must go. Do I have to? Yes.

People put themselves in danger for many reasons or for reasons they invent. Think of the collective madness of war, high-speed motor racing, mountaineering. I am sure my link with the past is real. Perhaps we all have them. I am special only because I was lucky enough to become aware.

I am so grateful to you for keeping the silence I asked for. Otherwise I could not have reached this point.

Loving you. Hope we'll meet again!'

He knew the last sentence was an example of Julie's humour but he was in no mood for even a smile. He was vastly relieved that she hadn't asked him not to follow. What then would he have done? Probably ignored the request, though he had no idea what he could achieve in that way. He knew that Julie must remain unaware of his presence and that he could not intervene unless her life was in extreme danger. Even in such a case he wondered if she would want him to interfere. He had anticipated the situation by making sure his car was ready and had put in provisions for a long night. Though there was little snow being carried, the wind was now strong enough to impede his walk to the car. He wondered what road conditions would be like and whether he could reach London. A normal two-hour journey might easily take twice as long. One good thing, he muttered to himself grimly, was that there would be little traffic. You'd have to be a bit crazy to be on the road tonight.

CHAPTER FORTY-NINE

---•◆•---

Julie's anxiety through the day, increasing by the hour, had been caused by the possibility that the trains would not be running. She had banked on travelling by rail but had not expected to be leaving in such wild weather. The worst of it had not reached the west as she walked to the station, but the gusts of wind caused her to falter several times. It was with enormous relief that she found the trains running to schedule and as hers pulled away she was confident that nothing further would obstruct her. The carriage was warm and she was forced to take off two items of the highly insulating clothing she was wearing. To avoid dwelling on the hours to come, which she was sure would prejudice the outcome, she traced the history of this project, beginning with her interest in the Science Group. That had been triggered by reading Rowan Selwood's book, which promoted the widening scope of science. Then there was the memorable evening when Paul's description of his early vision had triggered such a powerful feeling of familiarity. Her developing relationship with Peter had run a parallel course to her search, which had culminated with the discovery of Tillie, and looking back she could see how much the two were connected. Without that journey she supposed she and Peter would have just been ordinary lovers. Well, that wouldn't have been so bad. Her discoveries provided an unusual focus, but had also at times been a threat to the relationship. Julie had frequently been disappointed by what she saw as scepticism displayed by Peter right up to the discovery that Tillie was a long-ago relative. Did he have any faith at all that what she was about to do would yield any sort of enlightenment? Due to the moratorium she had imposed on relevant discussion she had no clue as to whether his attitudes had changed.

Behind the snow flurries the lights of London began passing and they were soon drawing in to an almost deserted Paddington Station. Her train had few passengers to give up and there was an early-morning feeling to the vast space, though it was still before eight in the evening. She paused on her way to the plaza and shut her eyes, trying to imagine the same place in the Victorian era. A feeling that could be described as time-related vertigo forced her to open her eyes as she contemplated the span of time from that era to the present. Generations, wars, revolutions lay between, yet here she was, a link in an ongoing genetic chain. She hurried from the station into the teeth of the storm. Snow was beginning to build in places but the drifts were being scattered by the howling gusts of wind. Julie was gripped by exhilaration as she battled her way along the familiar route to the outskirts of the park. She welcomed the empty streets. This was what she wanted.

By the time she reached the iron railings, notwithstanding the efficiently insulated clothing she had chosen, the cold was slipping in. As yet she was still comfortable and was determined not to rush her next step. In these conditions a mishap could undermine everything. She opened her rucksack and took out her carefully designed rope ladder. A powerful gust caught it as it unfolded and she had to grip it tightly to prevent it being blown away. During the next calm she hung the ladder over the top of the fence so that it afforded footholds on either side. In her mind she went over the series of steps that would take her over. Left foot here, right hand there, hold the top of the railing, one foot over. It should work. At the top, as she straddled the spikes, the wind gusted and she had to grip the ironwork and remain motionless. She watched the snow rush along the road, forming small whirlwinds. Then the wind dropped and with a few descending steps she was over. The lights of London reflected off the low scudding clouds, giving Julie a distant view of the dark frozen lake. There were now no barriers between her and her destiny.

Putting her arms through the railings she hauled up her rucksack, slinging it over her shoulder before setting off for the lake. Her rope ladder she left behind in case she needed it later. She occasionally stroked the rough bark of the bare sleeping cherry trees as she passed. She pictured the same scene when spring arrived. The trees in bloom, couples strolling in the warm sunshine. Shirtsleeves, summer dresses. The contrast amazed her. 'I will come then,' she promised the trees. The gusts must now be up to gale force, carrying with them both flakes and pellets of snow that stung her face. Had she expected such conditions, she would have brought a mask with a visor. The mournful calling of the wind in the tree tops was disorienting and she felt the first shards of fear, but it was a fear she had predicted and was ready for.

There were benches on the margin of the broad pedestrian path bordering the lake. Julie sat down to calm her emotions. It would be pointless to approach the ice until she had become settled, perhaps serene, but ten cold minutes passed before she felt the confidence to proceed. It was a high price to pay.

Julie stood and steadily and firmly approached the lake. She stepped onto the ice.

CHAPTER FIFTY

———◆———

Peter was relieved to reach the motorway, as snow was showing signs of building on the smaller roads. The M4 was weirdly quiet, as he expected, so driving was easy and he had time to think, though he knew the thoughts would yield no answers. Should he be following Julie? Would she get answers to her quest? Was she really experiencing something important with regard to mind and memory? And so on and so on as the miles passed. He was beyond Reading and making good time when an array of flashing blue lights ahead caused a momentary sinking of his heart, but thankfully the accident, for such it was, had occurred in the westbound carriageway. The sight brought home to him how easily he could be seriously delayed. In spite of the light traffic, the unusually wild weather might cause accidents. He was using the fast option for the windscreen wipers for most of the time now. Though his knowledge of music was very limited, 'Ride of the Valkyries' or maybe the driving rhythms of 'Pirates of the Caribbean' came to mind as appropriate as the snow swirled and the gale buffeted. To divert compulsive thoughts he tried humming them to himself as the miles passed.

The motorway ended and he entered urban west London. Bizarrely, it struck him that he might be liable to pay the congestion charge, though there was probably more congestion in Iceland than on London's roads tonight. Drifts were forming against buildings and the road surface was becoming white and treacherous. He had to slow down.

He reached the Outer Circle of Regents Park and slowed to a walking pace. He guessed where Julie would cross the boundary but had no idea how she would attempt this. He had imagined that he himself could park up against the railings and use the car to get over. He spotted what must be a rope ladder and pulled past it, driving over the kerb and close to the rails. Reality gripped his belly. She was clearly here, at the park. He slid over to the passenger seat and opened the nearside door, which was immediately ripped from his hands and flung open. Possessed now with a desperate urgency, he struggled into a pair of overtrousers and heavy sheepskin coat that he'd brought and scrambled over the bonnet onto the roof. Precariously using the car and railings top as footholds he leaped wildly across the boundary onto the deepening snow just inside the park. Struggling to his feet against the gale his whole focus now was getting to the lake edge and then round to the other side. The one thought that encouraged him was that surely there would be police patrol cars out and that if they came across his car and a rope ladder next to it they would investigate. Meanwhile, though weighed down by extra clothing, he had to run for his life, or for Julie's.

CHAPTER FIFTY-ONE

——•——

Thin curtains of snow were sweeping across the ice, swirling seemingly at random. The sight fascinated her but also threw her off balance. She found that if she concentrated on fighting the wind she could ignore the visual distraction. She had advanced four steps. The ice was holding and euphoric relief swept over her. Was this a dream? It seemed incredible that she was actually here. She brought her foot down sharply on the ice. She was startled to see a fracture line appear. The ice was not as thick as she'd expected. She must tread gently.

The cold seeping deeper into her body meant little. Each footstep was precious now; a gift from a hidden source taking her from the world she knew to something strange and wonderful. Minutes passed slowly. She reached the centre of the lake and turned slowly round. This was how she had envisioned it. This was what she had wanted. Alone and far from safety on a vast stage. Waiting.

There was no warning.

In an instant she was overwhelmed by an intense grief, the pain of which caused her to sink to her knees. She leaned forward and pressed her forehead against the ice and screamed in anguish. She had never known anything like this. The sorrow had no focus. From somewhere came a word. Endure. Endure. Over and over she repeated the word, willing the agony to fade. Her body lay on the ice, screwed into a tight ball. Relentless minutes passed. Then, when she felt she could endure no more, there came moments of relief when the pain lessened. During each such moment Julie tried to identify the source. Surely this was the pain of loss, greatly intensified, which had shadowed her life, but, unlike physical organic pain, was impossible to locate. She began to relax as the pain faded in long pulses. Then, as suddenly as it had arrived, it had gone. She rose unsteadily to her feet. Was what she had experienced the closing circle; a grief previously supressed that she had to feel? The cold had penetrated deep into her body and she knew her thoughts were becoming muddled. She tried to concentrate on her one aim. To reach the place at the edge of the lake where she had once stood. As she stumbled on, the whirling snowflakes took on shapes that came and went. There were people on the shore playing and dancing and there were voices shouting and laughing. She must reach them, but she was becoming dizzy and fell every few steps. Eventually she resorted to crawling, which method enabled her to get within three metres of the bank, at which point disaster struck. The ice around the edges of the lake had been broken the day previously and though the water had refrozen, Julie's weight was too much for it. Though her consciousness was fading she realised with a sharp poignant sadness that the cold, combined with the water, was probably going to kill her. She flailed desperately with her arms and sank until she touched the bed of the lake, which was soft and closed round her feet. There were some large pieces of ice floating, the remains of the original cover. She tried to use them to lever herself forward, at the same time pushing with her legs. She managed to get her arms onto the bank but doubted her ability to haul herself clear. She lay still, listening to the gale that seemed increasingly remote as the minutes passed and her body warmth seeped away. From nowhere there came a low-pitched chuckle inside her head. That's my laugh, she thought. How is someone else doing it? It came as a flash to her dimming brain. Tillie herself could be near, and as that realisation came she felt a powerful presence alongside. Fur rubbed across her face and she felt her coat seized and pulled strongly. Someone or something was trying to help her from the water. The pull continued and Julie made a last effort to raise her body to aid the would-be rescuer. She inched clear and lay listening to the low laughter. In the distance, she heard a dog barking.

She croaked. 'I'm dying. Don't I get to see the long tunnel and a light at the end?' She was weeping now, feeling pangs of self pity.

The laughter paused.

A voice echoed in her head from somewhere unknown. Tillie's?

'This will be better. This is my gift to you'.

At once she was free in a limitless ocean. Free of body, there was no sight or sound. Understanding flooded her mind. How did she not know all this before? She realised with wonder that this mind, whatever it was, existed in a different reality. She was in touch with the living universe and linked to other entities. Here was meaning. Here was love.

Somehow, for a moment in time, she had been released from all care and pretence so her naked soul could be bathed in pure compassion. This, finally, was why she had come. She subsided into a state of complete serenity.

The gift was over. Her body felt warm and this she knew marked its final minutes. She felt at peace and profoundly content. The smile on her face was now literally frozen, and during the short lapses in the gale, flakes of snow settled on her lips and eyelids. Her pulse weakened; then weakened more. Then stopped.

CHAPTER FIFTY-TWO

H
ad it not been for the dog running joyfully alongside, in circles
and with occasional forays into the snow flurries, Jim Prescott
would probably have spent the evening at home in the warm. He
couldn't imagine anyone out for trouble in this exceptional weather.
The dog, a Siberian Husky that Jim was looking after for a friend, was
obviously in his element. The friend was on a long vacation, actually at
Her Majesty's pleasure; something Jim, as a security officer, kept quiet
about. Jim was living in a lodge within London Zoo and his duties
involved the boundaries of the zoo and Regent's Park, which suited
Jake the husky well, with space to run as well as the bonus of finding
new scents left every day by visitors. He was also able to engage most
evenings with long howling conversations with the zoo's wolves. Since
the gale was blowing as hard as ever and a blizzard was beginning, Jim
couldn't imagine many scents being available that night, so he was
surprised when during a lull, Jake suddenly stood as if alerted, then
bounded off towards the lake. It remained a mystery ever after as to
what message Jake had received, but the consequences began soon
enough.

Jake returned quite soon and began barking. He also ran a short
distance along his original track and back, so it was clear to Jim that he
was supposed to follow the dog. When they reached the lake Jim was
shocked to see a body lying motionless beside the broken ice of the
lake. Jim saw that it was a woman and that were she to be left, there
would soon be little to locate her. In these conditions it was, he
thought, impossible to detect either breath or pulse and the quicker he
could summon emergency aid the better. He called 999, requested the
ambulance service and tried to explain the situation quickly.

'No, I'm not sure if she's breathing. I'm a security officer. Location
Regent's Park by the lake. I have a female, perhaps about early thirties,
in a hypothermic condition. I urgently need an ambulance.'

There was a pause.

'Caller. An ambulance has been despatched. I need to give the driver instructions.'

'Tell the driver to go to the park gate adjacent to Baker Street. I will meet them there but they may get there before me. Tell them to wait and I will unlock the gates so they will be able to get closer to the casualty.'

'Understood. Meanwhile if you can prevent further heat loss do so, but do not attempt to warm the patient.'

'Okay that and thank you.'

The only cover Jim had was a cape, which he unfolded and tried to wrap around Julie, but the wind was making it difficult and tucking it under her body as best he could he decided it was more important to get to the gate. He gave Jake a firm order to stay and set off. The dog seemed to have an understanding of the situation and settled down in the snow to wait.

CHAPTER FIFTY-THREE

Had Peter crossed the fence a few minutes earlier the two men would have met. As it was, Peter caught sight of Jim just before he disappeared in the direction of the west gates. Completely puzzled by the apparition and not knowing whether now to be less or more concerned about Julie, Peter decided to follow his original plan, which meant heading in the opposite direction to that of the stranger. Unused to running hard in heavy clothing, he tripped and fell twice before catching sight of Julie. His first glimpse as he approached gave him the shuddering shock that occurs when worst fears are realised. As he approached, a large dog, a husky, sprang to its feet. Shaking snow from its fur it stood silently regarding Peter, apparently not at all put out by the appearance of another human. The dog raised no objection to Peter as he knelt by Julie, coming forward in fact to sniff the newcomer. Peter went through the same thoughts as Jim had and reached the same conclusion. That Julie was hypothermic and was possibly technically dead. How the figure he had seen had come across Julie he couldn't imagine but it was likely that the person was the owner of the husky and that help would be forthcoming. Should he ring the emergency number? It could do no harm. In answer to his query he was told that yes, the situation had already been reported and an ambulance was on its way. Peter was given the same warning not to warm Julie and with that he had to be satisfied. He took off his heavy jacket and laid it over the cape which had clearly been an attempt to delay freezing. He looked at Julie's face and her smile brought tears. He wanted to keep hope alive but he knew there was a possibility that this was how her quest would end. Anger and sorrow fought for space with self-reproach in his mind. He wondered what she had experienced and whether it had been worth the risk on a night like this. He became aware again of the wind as it roared through the trees, bringing heavier snow.

The husky had settled again and Peter was brushing snow clear from Julie when he saw with relief the blue flashing lights on the far side of the lake, apparently inside the park. He wondered now about his own position. He would have to offer an explanation for Julie's state and his presence. The lights halted and Peter could only imagine voices and doors opening and closing, which the wind completely muted. It wasn't until the group from the ambulance arrived that their voices could be heard. There were two paramedics with a stretcher, who went straight to Julie to make an assessment. There was also a man who, having been greeted by the dog, turned to Peter.

'I'm assuming you know this lady,' he shouted.

Peter nodded, 'She's my partner.'

'Is there any point in asking what happened?'

'I've only just arrived,' Peter yelled, realising how ridiculous that sounded. 'It's a long story,' he added.

The medics had quickly rolled Julie onto the stretcher and the small group set off towards the ambulance through the blizzard. Jim leaned over to Peter to make himself heard.

'The police will want a word with both of us, I think. They're also on their way.'

A possible sudden death; maybe an assault. Would he be under suspicion? Of course. The job of the police entails thinking in that way.

Peter was able to discover Julie's destination before the ambulance roared off into the storm. The paramedics had been encouraging. Apparently 70 to 80 percent of patients recovered from severe hypothermia if treated quickly. A second police car joined the first, which had been waiting behind the ambulance. Jim and Peter were invited into the separate vehicles, both of which offered respite from the weather by way of quietness and warmth. The husky was content to settle again.

Peter did his best to explain Julie's mission, accepting the obvious disapproval of the two police officers and feeling uncomfortably like an errant schoolboy. Clearly he should have prevented his partner from executing her crazy plan. He related his journey and pointed out that his car was parked further along the road next to the fence and would certainly still be warm from his drive. He added that Julie's rope ladder, her way of entering the park, was still in place. They drove to where Peter's snow-covered car was parked, and having given the officer his contact details Peter was cleared to set off for the hospital. He would like to have taken Jim's details and hoped the police could supply them later. Letting the ambulance into the park had saved what may have been crucial time. Peter had no idea how Jim had achieved that.

His present task was to find his way to the Royal Free Hospital with only help from an A-to-Z of London. The roads were becoming slippery and many of the road names had disappeared under a coating of snow. It was a strange journey, and he was relieved to see the reassuring hospital lights.

CHAPTER FIFTY-FOUR

———◆———

The man on duty at main reception was reassuring and asked Peter about the weather as he entered decorated with unmelted snow.

'Just joking, sir. It's actually giving us a bit of a quiet night.'

'People with any sense are staying in of course,' said Peter ruefully. 'My partner's not one of them. She's been brought in with hypothermia. I'm not sure where I should go.'

'Really! I'm sorry to hear that. If you go over to A and E, they'll give you any information that's available, but that may not be much yet. Good luck.'

And this had been the case. Julie had been taken to somewhere on the third floor and that was all that was known at that moment. The receptionist at A and E would let the staff at Julie's location know of his presence and hopefully someone would come to update him soon. Peter began what he knew was going to be a long wait. He rang the school to leave a message that he wouldn't be in the next day, though he suspected that Elmbridge might be one of many schools closed. He began to absorb the strange ambience of a casualty waiting area: a place haunted by small but sometimes major disasters. The only other occupant was soon called through into the inner rooms and corridors of the hospital, leaving Peter alone with a pile of uninteresting magazines. Half an hour of worried inactivity later he decided one or two of the magazines were preferable to complete tedium, though the tedium, edged as it was by sharp anxiety, made concentration difficult. He spent quite a bit of time imagining the worst-case scenario. A member of the hospital staff would come over to him and sympathetically announce, 'She didn't make it I'm afraid,' as in so many films he had seen. So it was a relief when a nurse entered the area and called his name with a smile. She walked across and sat down, still thankfully smiling.

'I gather you're a friend of Julie Copeland.'

179

Peter nodded.

'Well there's no definite news and won't be for some time. She is undergoing a procedure, which will slowly warm her body. I expect you realise that she was in a deep hypothermic state on arrival. All her bodily functions had ceased, which means that at some point the doctors will attempt to restart her heart. Statistically there's a very good chance of full recovery but cases vary of course.'

The nurse paused, which Peter interpreted as a chance to ask any questions.

'What are the possibilities of brain damage in such cases?' It seemed the obvious question, but he had to ask it.

'I can only say from my limited experience and from reading that many people suffer no permanent brain damage, though they may be a bit disoriented at first and quite possibly have no recall of how they became frozen. Can you get home for the rest of the night?'

'Very doubtful. Julie and I live in Gloucester. It would be hazardous. I think I'll just stay in here.'

'Well it's not very comfortable but at least it's warm. I can't give you much of an estimate on time except it will be tomorrow morning earliest.'

'I'll be fine. I'm good at napping.'

Left alone, Peter felt calm for the first time since leaving Gloucester. Somewhere in the building competent people were trying to bring Julie back to life. He would wait and hope. He filled the hours by forcing himself to read the dog-eared magazines, occasionally napping for ten minutes and going through his pre-running stretches. Daylight arrived with Britain facing the aftermath of the storm. The hospital was waking up and casualties began arriving in the waiting room. Not surprisingly some of these were directly connected to the weather conditions. There had been many falls.

After letting reception know, Peter went to the cafe for breakfast, though it was fluid he most needed. As a runner he was usually aware of any sign of dehydration but the long night had led him to neglect fluid intake. There was no news for him back in the waiting room so his wait resumed. He heard several accounts of weather-related incidents and engaged in occasional chats with patients or their friends and relatives. He was getting used to this new life when it ended with a jolt. One of the reception staff called him over.

'A doctor will be coming to see you in a few minutes so you should go through the double door, which we'll open. There are seats in the corridor. You shouldn't have to wait long.'

Peter could not discern whether the news was good or bad and he knew he shouldn't ask. But all the muscles in his midriff had tightened and he suddenly desperately wanted to know one way or the other. He passed through the doors that had been swallowing people all morning and sat down, hands gripping the underframe of the seat as if he was on a white-knuckle ride at a theme park. For five tense minutes he watched life in the corridor. Nurses came and went, orderlies pushed trollies, three figures passed dressed in theatre scrubs, but Peter knew immediately when a doctor appeared with a particular body language that his wait was almost over. There was no message in the doctor's expression. Peter started to rise but the doctor waved him back.

'Mr Joy?'

CHAPTER FIFTY-FIVE

———•———

They walked hand in hand through the ornamental cherry trees, now in glowing blossom. Everything was just as Julie had imagined and promised herself in the depths of the storm. People strolled in the early summer sunshine, glad to be wearing their cheerful light clothes. The faintest of breezes carried warmth and a multiplicity of scents through the trees and across the lake. Shouts and laughter drifted from the various boats out on the water. Julie and Peter had initially walked along inside the fence to the place Julie thought had been her crossing point. Here they stood for a time taking in the scene.

'When you think about that night, this seems a paradise,' said Julie. 'Is this really the same place?'

Peter nodded. He was thinking how different had been their experiences. Julie with her determination to carry out her mission; he full of fear for her. The amazing feelings of relief and gratitude that had all but overwhelmed him on hearing that she was alive had never left him, were in fact renewed daily and today, here, they were intense. This was to be their last expedition to Regent's Park and surroundings. Today Peter would learn of the two events that had occurred that night of which Julie had clear memory. Everything else, from the spot they were standing at now, was a blank so far. Although not the only purpose of the visit, they had wondered whether coming here might help Julie recall whatever had happened in the blanks. In the same way and for the same reasons that preceded the event, she had delayed any discussion of her two experiences. Peter again had been asked to exercise patience because, she had explained, what had occurred needed careful thought before being discussed.

As they neared the wide path skirting the lake, Julie paused and pointed to a bench.

'I have this feeling that I waited there. Oh, it's so frustrating. Like those brief flashes from a dream. Let's sit there a bit. Perhaps something will come back.'

An elderly man was sitting at one end of the bench. As Peter and Julie arrived he got up to go.

'Oh, please don't go on our account,' said Julie. 'We're on a mission. Maybe you can help us.'

'How's that then?' asked the man, sitting down again, a mixture both of suspicion and interest in his voice.

The three sat in silence – Peter and Julie gazing out at the lake, the stranger wondering what would come next.

'Well?' he enquired eventually.

'We've come up from Gloucester today to sit here,' said Julie.

This was such an unexpected statement that the man began chuckling.

'That's a long way to come to sit on a park bench,' he said.

'Mm. The last time we were here was the day of that great storm. You remember, from the east?'

Peter listened, fascinated. What was she up to?

'Yes, it was like the old days when we had proper winters.'

'Do you live near here?' asked Peter, hoping that changing the subject was a good idea.

'You have to be joking. Mind, I used to. That's why I come here sometimes. My wife and three children fairly lived in this park. The kids went on the boats at the children's pond. We all went out on this lake in one of those big rowing boats. Good Victorian vessels they were. Clinker-built with lovely ironwork. Not like those things out there now that'll stop dead if you stop rowing. The old ones would glide maybe twenty yards.'

'Do you have to come far?' asked Julie, pleased that the old man was enjoying reminiscing.

'Brixton's where I live now. It's a change for me here to see some white people. You know I walked past a primary school during the lunch hour last week. There were only four white kids in the playground. They all seemed happy enough and when you closed your eyes and listened you'd never know what colour any of them were. That's hopeful isn't it?'

Julie and Peter both nodded agreement.

'What you said just then is beautiful. I wish more people would shut their eyes occasionally,' said Julie. 'Did you ever hear about the disaster in Victorian times when the ice here gave way?' she continued.

'I think my dad talked about it when I was a kid. That's why we couldn't go skating. But I did go out once,' he chuckled. 'I must have been about three. Mum was holding my hand so I could walk on the ice at the edge. I was longing to go out on that great empty expanse and kept pestering. I promised to stay at the edge if she let go and she gave in. I was off like a shot out into the middle. It was amazing looking all round so far from the shore. Like being on a huge flat stage and me the only actor.'

Julie drew a sudden breath and exclaimed, 'Yesss.'

The man hardly noticed, his focus so far in the past.

'That great feeling only lasted a moment though, what with everyone shouting: my parents, two park keepers and a few others. Could have drowned, I suppose, but I never forgot the experience. Well, nice to have met you. I've got some walking to do. Good luck with your mission. I don't suppose I've helped much.'

'You'd be surprised,' replied Julie as the man set off towards the boat house.

As soon as he was out of earshot Julie turned to Peter, her eyes sparkling.

'I got this flash when he was describing being out in the middle. It was just how I felt, looking around with no references nearby. For a few moments I was the only living being on earth. Anyway, just like that man the sensation lasted only a moment before it was eclipsed by my first experience, the first of the two that are clear. I've had these few months to think about them and you've been patient. Well, here goes. Are you ready?'

Julie took a deep breath.

'This powerful feeling of grief hit me like a hammer-blow, and for no obvious reason. I was knocked to the floor begging for oblivion, which didn't come. I was face down, staring at the ice and somehow knowing I had to endure the pain. My tears were flowing onto the ice. I thought maybe they would melt it and that caused me to laugh hysterically in between screaming. The wild laughing and shrieking was the only way to get relief from the pain. There was no focus to the grief. It was as if I had become grief. I've no idea how long it lasted. My body twisted and turned on the ice. Waiting, and of course getting colder. The first tiny bit of relief came but, like a throbbing toothache, the pain returned. So it continued, gradually subsiding. Then a blank. The next I remember I'm grasping the bank knowing I'm about to die. I realise the ice has broken and I'm still half submerged and feel I'm slipping back into the water. I don't want to drown but I can't stop slipping. In my head there is this gentle laughing and I think of Tillie. Something grabs my clothing and pulls strongly. With that help I edge up onto the bank. I'm feeling warm and I've read that's what happens near the end. I'm not frightened though I know my life is nearly over. I think about the tunnel you hear about, with a light at the end. I want it. I ask why I can't see it.'

Julie paused, a distant look on her face. Peter had listened, fascinated. The sounds of the park faded and they sat alone while Julie prepared to describe what happened next. The first time she had done so since the storm.

'I heard a quiet laugh, which sounded just like mine. I thought in fact, "that's me." Then a voice; is it mine or am I hearing Tillie herself? I hear "This will be better. This is my gift to you." What happened then I can't really find words for but I'll get as close as I can.

'I am free from the physical universe but aware of it. I see and hear nothing in the usual way but the awareness is intense and I understand. Not as we usually think of it but more a state of understanding. The universe is alive. There is meaning everywhere. In joy but also in pain, loss and sacrifice. I realise that I am still an entity and can think but no longer have a name. Do I have will? I think about our moon and experience its massiveness as it glides. I embrace the earth. I am conscious, but I am sharing my consciousness, and I am part of the consciousness of other entities. There are the most amazing vibrations. I am part of this music. I want to explore, to experiment in this amazing existence but I know I'm an infant here and have to let go. Different states flow by me or through me and I gently fade into a serenity I can only describe as oceanic. I exist in a timeless infinity of peace and love. Somehow I know when I have to leave. There is no regret or sorrow as I become aware of my body. I am lying in a bed. I begin to weep with a joy I cannot describe. There are people around me who are concerned. I try to extend the peace and love that has stayed with me. Can I share the gift? I close my eyes and let myself be reclaimed by the world. I realise soon that I am in a hospital and that the event is over; that what I have left is a memory that I am somehow able to keep; a gift.'

There was silence. Julie was aware of Peter gazing at her and brought herself back to Regent's Park on a pleasant spring morning. Were these tears of happiness running down her cheeks?

'What do you make of that?' she finally asked. 'Was it real or did I imagine or invent it all?'

Peter was trying to absorb the events Julie had just described. He looked out at the lake again, the stage on which Julie had fought the storm to meet the destiny she had predicted. He thought again, as he had many times, about the whole series of events that had led up to the final drama here, and the reasons he had sometimes been sceptical.

'Well?' Julie was waiting, but laughing gently, knowing the answer.

Peter began carefully. 'First there was the dream image with linked emotions of sadness and loss. Spontaneous, repeated and never forgotten. Then the image identified through a picture, so tied you to a particular disaster of which you knew nothing. A tragedy among millions of tragedies. You discover you are descended seven or eight generations back to a woman bereaved by the disaster. Does the call you discern actually exist outside your mind? Was there a circle needing closure? Your solution is to be where it would matter at a time that would matter. You predict an event and your two experiences surely, by their otherworldliness, justify your expectations. We may never understand what has happened and possibly aren't expected to, but I personally don't doubt the reality of it.'

Julie had listened thoughtfully to Peter's answer and felt there was nothing to add. Maybe they would go on discussing that night for years. Would they ever get any sort of explanation? And would they want to? They strolled across the bridges by the boat house to the spot where Julie's mission had ended and from which, so long ago, Tillie and George had witnessed a terrible tragedy. They gazed out over the water for several minutes, lost in their own thoughts. By a fence that enclosed an area bordering the lake there was a straggling line of daffodils, well past their prime. Julie walked over to them and took a small envelope from her pocket and shook the contents into her palm; small dry flakes. She passed the envelope to Peter, who read Julie's neat lettering: 'Dafydd's Gift to Tillie. Circa 1875.' Walking along the row of dying plants, she scattered the ancient remains as evenly as she could.

She smiled at Peter. 'I'm sure she would approve.'

www.ingramcontent.com/pod-product-compliance
Lightning Source LLC
Chambersburg PA
CBHW030256270626
47156CB00022B/2779